MW00879000

TWISTING

EVERY

WAY

Amy Sutphin

A Twisted Realm Novella

ISBN: 978-0-578-94720-4 (Paperback)

ISBN: 978-0-578-94718-1 (Ebook)

Any references to historical events, real people, or real places are used fictitiously. Names, characters, and places are products of the author's imagination.

First Ebook Edition 2020.

First printing edition 2021.

Chapter One

The night sky glowed with a thousand stars, one for every living soul. Emya stood, head thrown back, strands of her long, dark hair, pulled away by the wind, wisped gently around her. Her wide, brown eyes moved across the sky, as she wondered which of the stars had not been there the night before. Had she known what was going to happen, she would have looked up at the sky more.

The buzzing voice of the chief councilor droned on, unintelligible to Emya. Grim-faced onlookers clicked their tongues disapprovingly but Emya ignored them and continued to gaze up at the sky. She would look anywhere other than at those somber expressions watching her with a mixture of pity and disdain as she stood before the two caskets.

After a time, the speeches and rituals were finished, and the chief counselor ended the ceremony. As the crowd dispersed, Emya stood motionless, trapped by indecision. To follow the crowd felt cowardly. She deserved to witness what came next; it was her fault.

When the crowd disappeared beyond the shadow of the squat village houses, four burly men were left behind to finish the task. As the caskets disappeared below the dirt, a heavy weight lifted from her shoulders and settled permanently in her stomach. They were gone and she was well and truly alone.

A firm hand clapped her shoulder. She tore her eyes away from the graves to gaze dully into the stern face of Councilor Hai.

"The mourning gathering has started, Emya. Why don't you go and eat?" He'd never spoken so softly to her. It was almost sympathetic, but he couldn't quite mask the twang of disapproval. No one would miss her if she did not go to the mourning gathering. It was not for her, but for the few people who had liked her mother and father despite their having a child such as her. The others would gossip and speculate on what would become of her. Yet, if she did not attend for at least a few minutes she would be labeled an uncaring daughter and contemptuous of the village traditions. This would translate to crueler treatment, scolding, and further punishment.

Her boots softly scraped the dirt as she trudged up the path from the cemetery to the cobbled village street. Not even the soft calls of the nocturnal birds that lived in the thatch dared to break the eerie silence. Strange though it was, Emya felt it fitting. On either side of her sat squat, stone houses with narrow, canvas windows and roofs thatched with long, serrated grass. Built closely together for protection from the occasional violent storm, the structures were sturdy, warm in the winter and cool in the summer. Nestled indistinctly among the others, close to the village square, one house stood, its windows dark and empty. Emya stopped, transfixed by an ominous mark that had been carved into the door —the mark of tainted blood.

Painted with animal fat mixed with umber and red ocher to indicate murder, her parents' murder, as though anyone in the village didn't know, it was a warning to stay out. The tainted blood contained an evil that could infect anyone exposed. But Emya already had evil in her blood.

The villagers said she must have gotten it, the bad blood, from her parents, but her mother always insisted Emya hadn't. Emya never knew for sure. They had never shown any symptoms of the condition. So, it didn't matter if she went in the house or not, but she didn't want to give the fearful villagers another reason to mistreat her.

On to the village center she went, dragging her feet with every step. Fewer than eighty people lived in the village and the largest structure, the council hall, could barely hold that number. When Emya slipped in, she found nearly twenty villagers scattered around in small groups, their heads together as they whispered in tones that sounded more conspiratorial than mournful.

After the last tragedy that struck the village, a house collapsed killing a family of five, the whole village had turned out for the funeral gathering; the hall was packed to bursting. This small turnout came as no surprise.

Wending through the hall, her gaze was fixed firmly on the long table at the end with steaming dishes that had been brought by the villagers. From the tones of conversation, she could tell who was there because they wanted to be and who was there because they felt obligated. Most were the latter. Serving herself a small plate, she sat alone in the corner, facing the wall.

What happened next was an odd parade of unusual behavior. An old woman shuffled past, patting her on the shoulder as she went by. Then a man stood stoically before her and said in a stiff voice, "My condolences." He was followed by a woman with a small girl clinging to her skirt. At her mother's beckoning, the girl placed a small bundle of dark purple flowers next to Emya's plate. Suspicious and unsure of how to react, she sat stiffly in her chair, ignoring each act of sympathy.

When she finished what little she could stomach, she rose to her feet. Without knowing where she was supposed to go, she lingered in the corner. From the moment she'd found her parents dead she'd been unable to think further ahead than the next few minutes. Now uncertainty competed for her attention. What was she supposed to do next? Where would she live? How could she manage her condition? How would she protect herself? In a lifetime that had been marred with questions, it seemed now that her future had been swallowed whole by them.

Her feet took her past the tables and their murmuring occupants. She would go back to her house, break-in, curl up in her bed and never leave it. She was almost to the doors when a tall, grim, older woman stepped in her way.

"You must be tired," said Councilor Kamala.

"I'm going home." The words slipped out before she could think better. Kamala glared at her, features twisting in disdain at Emya's defiance.

"You can't go in there, it's contaminated. You must come live with me for the foreseeable future."

So that was to be her fate. To be under the thumb of the one person in the village who her parents had protected her from the most. Though Kamala could do nothing while Emya was considered a child, she knew Kamala would see her exiled, or worse, the moment she turned twenty. Following the woman out into the night, they walked in silence through the dark, silent village.

The only signs of life were the flickering torches of the night watch.

Flat, sprawling grasslands surrounded the village, ensuring that no visitor or invader could sneak up on it as long as the guards kept vigilant. In accordance with tradition, each of the councilors lived at one of the cardinal points. Kamala lived on the easternmost point in a house that stood alone, away from the rest, which represented her position of authority, as well as the risks she and the other village leaders assumed — or at least that's what Emya had always been told. She never understood exactly what that meant. As far as she knew, nothing very dangerous ever happened in the village, let alone something that put the leaders at more risk than the rest.

Kamala opened her house's only door and led Emya inside. It was dark and unfamiliar. Emya shuffled behind Kamala, bumping her toes against furniture, corners, and walls. Usually, Emya was adept at getting around in the dark. Wood was hard to come by and the grass they had in abundance burned too quickly for a decent fire. Once a year, as a village, candles were made and then hoarded, used only sparingly. Emya could move around the village and her own house in the dark with ease. Not so in here.

Frustrated by her fumbling, Kamala grabbed Emya by the collar of her dress and pulled her along in the dark to a little room in the back of the house. Pushing her in, she shut the stiff weave of grass that constituted a door. With a sigh, Emya felt along the wall until she came to a corner, then another, then another, then the door again. It was tiny, no bigger than a closet.

On the floor was a mat, a blanket and a pillow, which took up all but a small sliver of the width of the room. In a corner at the foot of the makeshift bed was a small wooden chest. She knelt and ran her hand over it. Ornate carvings decorated the lid. An heirloom, it must have been in Kamala's family for a long time. She was touched the woman would let her use it. Gently, she lifted the lid and felt through the contents. Clothes and a pair of shoes. Not hers, no one would risk going into her house to get her belongings, but they would fit.

Exhausted—she had been for quite some time—and with nothing more to do, she fell into the makeshift bed and drifted into a deep, dreamless sleep.

Cries of terror and panic woke Emya. Bolting upright, she scrambled over the floor. Confused, shaking in terror, she was unable to recall where she was. The acrid, choking smell of scorched thatch filled her lungs. Coughing, she crawled along, feeling for the wall, then the door. On the other side of the door was only black. Using the wall to leverage herself to her feet, she felt along it until she came to a small room filled with flickering light. She remembered whose house it was. Shame it hadn't caught fire.

Striding the short distance to the thickly woven grass door, she pushed it open and looked around wildly. Three houses were burning and villagers were running pell-mell. Some attempted to fight the fires, while others ran past Emya, fleeing the burning village for the relative safety of the steppe. Poised to run, she was about to follow the villagers away from the danger when another shrieking scream pierced the air, then another. From the dark, villagers came running back into the chaos and past the burning houses.

From her vantage, Emya could not see what they were running from, and she did not linger long to find out. Spiriting away from Kamala's house and into the village proper the heat from the burning houses scorching her. The narrow paths between the houses were clogged with villagers trying to escape. Emya didn't know which way to go, but the crowd pushed her towards the south.

She tried to see what danger lay behind her and found nothing but panicked people. Struggling through the sea of bodies, someone pushed her into a cart. Unable to push her way back into the crowd, and afraid of falling and being trampled, she waited for them to pass.

The crowd thinned. Emya stepped back onto the path, following the stragglers. Out of the corner of her eye, she saw something propelled through the air towards her. She dived out of the way just as a man landed on the ground in a heap. Stepping over him, she cut left and dashed through a narrow path between two houses and emerged onto a path running northwest. Mud slipped under her feet. Her skin tingled as though there was lighting in the air. The hair on her arms stood up. Somehow, she'd reached the village square. It was deserted.

The light from the flaming houses lit up the horizon, though she could see nothing in the dark around the square. Silence fell over her like a heavy blanket. For a moment she feared she'd gone deaf, then a tapping noise of heavy boots on stone startled her. She whirled around. A tall, dark figure sauntered towards her through the houses.

Frozen, she watched the man unsheathe a great sword as he closed the distance between them. As though generating a great storm, lightning cracked from the blade. Each flash illuminated the beast of a warrior. She stumbled back and fell. The warrior loomed over her, sword held aloft.

The muddy path blubbered as air escaped with every clumsy step. Emya's feet slid around in boots too big for her, but she hurried along as fast as she could. Eyes cast down, rain drizzled on her hunched shoulders and soaked hair, dripping off the end of her nose. Her neighbors' feet moved away as she passed. Her destination was the village square, though she wished to go nowhere near it. Kamala had a task for her to complete, and to fail to do so would ensure a punishment.

Muddy paths gradually gave way to warn cobble paving. When she reached the edge of the square she halted. At the center of the largest open space in the village loomed an old well, the main water source for the village. Beyond the well was the council chamber—or the 'throne room,' as they were now to call it. The chamber was made of tall, black stone from a faraway mountain that their ancestors had harvested to create sanctuary and community. A sanctuary no more.

It never had been a sanctuary for Emya, but now the center of village life was the most avoided place in the little settlement, and Emya, the most avoided inhabitant, was sent to draw water from the well for the whole village. Several times a day, she found herself alone at the well. Eyeing the great, carved throne room doors, silent and still, from her perch at the edge of the paving, she hoped and prayed that they would remain closed as she scurried forward. An unsettling feeling gripped her. Her skin tingled and the hair on her arms stood up. A thick soup of energy radiated from the throne room.

Taking a deep, calming breath, she crossed the short distance to the well, picked up the coiled rope, tied her bucket, and tossed it in. The well was almost full from all the rain they'd had. She winced as the rope dug into her as she hauled the heavy bucket up.

The skin on her shoulders had been raw from repeated use. Adjusting the rope, she glanced at the throne room doors which still did not stir.

They called themselves the Kings, the men who'd conquered the village almost one month ago. Among other strange decrees, they'd forbidden the villagers from collecting water from any sources except the well. The collection of rainwater was forbidden, as were trips to the stream that flowed through the valley during the rainy season. Storing water in barrels also had been outlawed, a concerning change as the well would all but dry up in the coming dry season. She had no idea why they'd declared such an insane edict in a land where water was scarce most of the year.

The bucket scrapped and bumped the side of the well as she pulled it. Water sloshed back into the well, the splash echoing in the silent stillness.

A blood-curdling scream pierced through the silence. The rope dropped from her hands. Scrambling, heart pounding, she slid through the mud around the well and pushed her back against its bricks. Pressing her hands over her face, she trembled in terrified anticipation and waited.

Silence settled once more over the dreary village. Cautiously peeking over the well, she found the throne room doors still shut and the square empty but for herself. She stood slowly, keeping her eyes on the doors, and nervously wiping the mud off her pants as best she could. Her tunic was torn a little at the seam. An easy fix, but Kamala would be cross.

The rope had not fallen into the well, much to her relief. She picked it up, all but running the bucket up the well, ignoring the burning in her shoulder. When the bucket reached the edge of the well, she lifted it out, filled to the brim. Impossibly full. She tipped a little back in.

Hefting the bucket handle in both hands, holding it away so as not to bump it, she ambled back into the village. As she left the square behind and made her way deeper into the village, the inhabitants materialized, hurrying along on some errand or another, or standing around, leaning against their houses. Averting her eyes, she concentrated on the muddy path.

A woman worked outside her small, grey house, pulling weeds from the small garden of potatoes, carrots, and herbs. She looked up and scowled as Emya approached. Without speaking, Emya placed the bucket near the woman and turned to leave.

"Wait," the woman snapped. Arms crossed and shoulders hunched, Emya looked at the woman through her lashes.

"This is a lot of water. How did you get this much? I could never have done it. Not even my husband could have done this."

She should have dumped out more, but then the woman probably would have found some other fault in her work.

"I've been pulling a lot of water," Emya said with a shrug. "I've gotten good at it."

The woman stood and took a step forward, her hand slightly raised as if she intended to hit Emya but she thought better of it.

"Just go," she said, "but if something happens to my garden, I'll be seeing Kamala."

No one could prove there was anything wrong with the water. Anything could kill off her garden. Plants died, either eaten by bugs or sickness or in this case overwatering, because the rain had saturated the soil. Why the woman needed more water from the well was beyond Emya, but she could still be punished whether she was guilty or not.

Eager to be far from the irate woman, Emya

pivoted in the mud, then stopped, and stepped back. A beast of a man towered over her. He wore only a crudely-fashioned fur cloth around his waist. One of the older village men recognized the fur and said it came from an animal called a tiger. He had said that warriors who wore it had fought and killed the beast with their bare hands. The rest of his body was exposed, and his head, arms, legs, and chest were shaven to better display the patterns of scars and ink.

King Azo regarded her with cold blue eyes. She stumbled back into the garden. The woman stood behind her, frozen and fearful.

"Who are you?" King Azo demanded, gesturing lazily at Emya.

"Emya," she said, her voice so soft that she wasn't sure he'd heard her.

"Were you at the well just now?"

"Yes."

"She's the one I was telling you of," the woman cut in, eager to please.

"Quiet." With one powerful hand, he smacked the woman across the face, knocking her off her feet. She lay in a heap, unmoving. Emya stood in frozen, wide-eyed fear.

"We told all the villagers they must use the well, yet you are the only one who draws water from it. Why is that?"

Emya searched for her voice but it was gone. He tilted his head irritably. She sucked in a breath to speak.

"I go for them." She forced the words out in a ragged breath.

"You get the water for the whole village?"

She nodded.

"You could not. You do not have the strength. It would take all day and night, yet you do it in a few hours?"

"I don't get water for everyone," she lied. "Some go when I can't."

"No," he said. "They don't. We would know if they did. It's only you."

Emya clenched her jaw fearfully. She knew what he was implying, but she could not say it, no matter what. If the Kings knew, they'd use her. The councilors, according to Kamala, made it very clear no one was to tell the Kings what she was capable of. She glanced at the woman still lying on the ground. She had not headed the councilors decree, and now Emya would pay, one way or another.

"You don't know that you get the water for the whole village? You just do it?"

"I guess."

To her surprise, he nodded, as though he believed her. Maybe he really did.

"You will come to the throne room at sunset." He turned and sauntered off, leaving Emya dumbstruck. When he was out of sight, she glowered down at the woman who stirred and sat up.

"You told him," Emya said flatly.

"Yes, I did," she said defiantly, "and I was rewarded handsomely."

"I can see that."

"This," she touched her already bruising face, "is nothing."

She got to her feet and marched into her house, slamming the door pointedly behind her. Emya thought she heard a muffled sob.

She had no time or sympathy to spare for the woman. Instead, Emya began to consider the punishment they both would receive if the councilors learned of what had transpired. Trying to head it off, Emya trudged through the village in search of Kamala. At the very least, she had to tell her about the appointment with the Kings. Keeping her informed had become a priority for Emya. Kamala became very angry if Emya went anywhere without telling her. This was partially Emya's fault. The first chance she got after moving in with Kamala, she had snuck into her parent's house to retrieve some of her belongings. Kamala hadn't worried about where Emay was until she found Emya's mother's favorite necklace, which she promptly confiscated, and warned Emya of what would happen if she ever went anywhere without her permission. Emya hadn't seen her mother's necklace again, much to her discouragement.

Finding Kamala near the house of Councilor Hai, no doubt on her way to a secret council meeting forbidden by the Kings, Emya stopped her and explained what had happened, prudently leaving out that the woman had tattled on her to the Kings.

"You will finish your chores," Kamala said unsurprisingly. "And you had better do them quickly. The Kings will be angry if you're late."

And *she* would be angry if Emya didn't finish her chores, Kings or no Kings.

At sunset, tired and dirty, Emya hurried to the throne room. Perhaps Kamala thought the barbaric Kings wouldn't notice the grime; perhaps she hoped they would dismiss her for not being presentable.

As she approached the throne room, she futilely combed her fingers through her damp, knotted hair and wiped her face on her gritty sleeve. Few villagers had entered the former council chamber since the arrival of the Kings, and fewer had emerged.

She began to tremble with anxiety as she stood, deciding whether to knock. They might not hear it through the thick timber but barging in felt reckless. Determining it was better to be polite, even if the kings didn't recognize manners or common courtesy, she tapped on the door, waiting several moments, then slowly pushed it open.

The council room was more brightly lit than she had ever seen it. Huge torches blazed along the stone walls, and smoke and the stench of burning animal fat made the air heavy and thick. The Kings must have had to carry logs a great distance to keep these fires blazing. Wood was rare, almost too precious to burn.

All the tables had been removed and all of the chairs were gone except for two set on a platform crudely constructed of stone. Lounging on the makeshift thrones were the Kings. The unwelcome rulers regarded her with an intensity that stopped her just past the doors.

"Don't stand in the door. Come closer," Azo said. Beside him, Gabek-Fen grunted impatiently. The blunter of the two Kings, his more violent temper was a little more predictable than Azo's. She feared both Kings equally and did not care to move any closer. Though she knew she must comply, fear held her to the spot. Yet, seemingly against her will, she took a step forward, and then another.

"What is your name?" Asked Gabek-Fen, leaning forward and looking her up and down.

"Emya," she said, shrinking away from his hungry gaze.

"Emya, tell me, do you know how you are able to get water for the whole village? It's almost impossible to do that much work in one day."

He already knew the answer, and so did she, but she wasn't going to say it. All her life she'd been told never to speak of it, her condition. The Councilors would kill her if she ever uttered the words, and the whole village would applaud them for doing so.

"I'm fast and strong. I've had a lot of practice," she said, feigning ignorance. Azo shook his head, his expression hardening with impatience. His piercing blue eyes seemed to gaze upon her thoughts. Emya shifted uneasily as they waited for her to tell the truth.

Relaxed though they appeared, she'd just witnessed how quickly they became violent. If she refused to answer truthfully they would hurt her. If she said the forbidden word, even after all these years, everything she'd been taught and the protection she'd built around herself from it would all be undone. She would no longer be safe under the mantle of denial.

"Magic." The word slipped off her tongue like a long-imprisoned man escaping into the night. Finally, free.

The Kings smiled.

"Your village doesn't like magic, do they?" Azo asked.

"No," she said.

"Why not?"

"It's evil. It makes people hurt people."

She could hear her mother's voice in her own, reciting the words she'd repeated to Emya any time her young daughter asked about magic.

"Oh? And it does that all on its own?"

Emya frowned. This was the question she'd pondered all her life, the question that would determine if she lived or died. Her mother always said her magic would destroy everything she hated, then everything she loved, and then eventually it would consume her. As long as she never used it, kept it bottled up deep inside, everyone would be safe. The villagers thought otherwise. They believed that one day her magic would burst out of her, its power slipping beyond her control, and destroy them all.

"I don't know," she said.

The Kings nodded.

"Magic is a powerful, destructive force," Gabek-

Fen said, a hungry gleam in his eyes.

"But it can also be used to build and create," Azo said. "We can teach you."

A muted whine like an injured animal drew Emya's fixed gaze away from the Kings. Huddled in a corner behind the thrones was a sickly pale young man with fever bright eyes. Strange, golden, fearful eyes. His long, matted hair stuck to his face, and his tattered, threadbare clothes hung from his skeletal frame.

"Ignore him!" Azo roared. Emya ripped her gaze away from the pitiable sight, pushing to the back of her mind an unsettling feeling she didn't quite understand or have time to analyze.

"From now on you will be our apprentice. We will train you to be a mage." Azo said, calm once more.

This decision had been made before she walked into the throne room. It had been made the moment they realized she was the only one pulling water from the well. Maybe even before that. She could not oppose the Kings, but she couldn't survive without protection if she started using magic.

"I can't," she said, gesturing desperately at the door. "Those people out there will kill me."

"They will never get the chance," Gabek-Fen growled.

"You must learn how to use your magic or it will kill you," Azo said. "And when you do, none of the villagers will be able to hurt you. They will fear you."

They already feared her, nothing could change that, and now the Kings were adding another possibility no one had ever suggested to her before- that she would lose her life following her mother's advice to keep her magic buried. Still, using her magic could destroy them all. All the people she hated. There was no one that she loved. Yet as much as she hated them, she didn't want to destroy them.

16

"I don't want to hurt them," she murmured.

Azo smiled and then spoke again. "You can use magic to make them love you, or ignore you, whatever you want. You can make your life better."

She wasn't sure she believed that, but if there was a chance it was true, then she could at least try. She had to do what was best for herself because no one else would.

"Alright," she said. "Then teach me."

The Kings smiled.

Chapter Two

Emya tore through the streets towards Kamala's house. An unsettling sight, the villagers murmured anxiously as she passed. When she arrived out of breath, Kamala stood up from the garden and gawked at her with a mixture of annoyance and alarm. Emya brushed past her and entered the house. She didn't have time to convince Kamala to let her do what she had to, though she was sure to face some opposition from the obstinate woman. The Kings had instructed Emya to gather her things and bring them back to the "castle." It was just a small house near the council chamber, but the villagers started calling it the castle after the Kings ordered it vacated for their own use. As far as Emya could tell, they rarely did much of anything there.

Inside Kamala's home, she hurried down the hall to her tiny room and then stopped in the doorway, suddenly unsure of what to take. Most of the possessions in her quarters technically didn't belong to her. Even though Kamala had no use for clothing that didn't fit her anymore, she had made sure that Emya knew none of it belonged to her.

"What are you doing?" Kamala huffed from behind her.

"I'm leaving," Emya said quickly, searching through the clothing chest where she'd stashed the few things that she did own. She wished Kamala hadn't been home. The woman wasn't likely to let her go without a fight.

Whack!

Emya fell forward from the force of the blow. The old woman could still pack a punch.

"You ungrateful swine! I take you in, give you food and clothing, and you think you can steal from me?"

Emya picked herself up, rubbing the back of her head.

"Fine," she said. "I won't take your clothes."

Emya pulled off her disgusting pants and tunic and put on the only clothing that was truly hers: the dress she'd worn on the day her parents died. Kamala watched with a mixture of fury and, if she wasn't mistaken, relief. Emya stuffed a small box and a ribbon that had belonged to her mother into her pocket.

"And where do you think you're going?" she asked as Emya pushed past her.

"I'm going to live with the Kings," she said. Kamala's face twisted into disgusted satisfaction.

"So, they've taken a fancy to you? Not surprising. Those filthy animals would want trash such as you. And you go running to them. Well, I hope they give you what you deserve."

Emya stared at her in shock. She meant some sort of salacious tryst, Emya was sure. She'd been accused of many things, but this was a first. Turning slowly from the repellent old woman she left the house. The door clicked as it swung shut behind her, never to be opened by Emya again.

~~*~*~*~*

A bead of sweat trickled down the small of Emya's back. She shivered and patted at her damp, grey tunic. The roaring fire in the center of the throne room scorched and blackened the jagged chunks of stone which the Kings had dug out of the chamber's floor and stacked in a ring to create a fire pit. The Councilors would never have allowed a fire in the council chamber. The smoke was already damaging the stone wall carvings that depicted important stories and events in the village's short history.

The Kings had no regard for this. Emya didn't either. She liked the way the room looked bathed in light. She never knew the stone could sparkle, giving the needle-thin carvings a life all their own.

One carving depicted a mighty warrior, sword held aloft, poised to defend the village against an undefeatable monster that once terrorized the land. Emya doubted the story, considering there were no other accounts of such creatures, but she'd always admired the carving. Men like the warrior didn't exist in the village anymore. As she stared at him the warrior's head turned slowly in the flickering light, his piercing gaze coming to rest on her. Startled, Emya fell off the stool in a heap. She picked herself up and looked at the carving again. The warrior was back to normal.

Emya righted the stool and settled onto it after smoothing her tunic and brushing her hair out of her face. Azo paced the width of the room, unaware of the carvings or his high-strung pupil. He was fiddling with

20

what appeared to be a wooden sphere with black gems set in it. The gems rolled in their sockets as he ran his fingers along them. Emya had been sitting there for some time, waiting for him to get on with the lesson. Ever since she'd started learning magic, strange things, like the moving carvings, happened in ever-increasing frequency. She would try to explain it away as a result of the excessive heat and burning of herbs that often made her dizzy, but she suspected there was more to it. The Kings said that her experiences were normal and would stop once she learned a little more.

The Kings, despite their size, were surprisingly quiet and stealthy. Azo's steps on the stone floor were silent. The only sounds in the council chamber were the crackling of the fire and the occasional whimper and hiccup from the corner where the ever-present shadow slumped against the wall in a heap.

Emya called him the Shadow in her head because she was forbidden from looking at him or talking to or about him. Yet he was always there, a shape she saw out of the corner of her eye. A gloomy presence just out of sight. A shadow.

It was not lost on her that the Kings treated him as the villagers treated her, worse in fact. At first, she felt sorry for him. Then she selfishly pushed those feelings aside so she could finally bask in the warmth of the Kings' favor. For the first time in her life she was wanted, encouraged, and treated with dignity. Embracing the sudden improvement of her circumstances, she no longer cared about what was happening to anybody else.

Azo stopped and tossed the object into the fire. Emya watched it burn. At first, she thought he'd gotten fed up with it and tossed it in out of anger, but the fire seemed to transform it from wood into bright yellow stone. The black gems twisted on their own in the flames.

Azo watched it until the stones stopped spinning. Then he reached into the fire with a grunt and pulled it out. Holding it in his hands, he motioned for Emya to take it. Opening her hand gingerly, the object fell into her palms. It was warm but it did not burn.

"What is it?" she asked as she turned it over and over. It was the size of a small loaf of bread and felt like no material she'd ever held, though it looked like stone now.

"That is an object of power. It can be used to focus magic and help you direct it as you desire, but you must be very careful. If you don't have the strength to stop the flow of energy it will draw your power, strength, and eventually your life from you." He took the object gently from her hands and placed it on a table, then sat down on the stool next to her.

"Have you been practicing?" he asked. Emya nodded. "Show me."

She took a deep breath. Magic was not what she imagined it to be. She'd always thought it was an explosion of power and destruction. That could happen, Azo had explained, but it was a very rare occurrence for someone properly trained. Channeling her magic to use at will seemed almost impossible. For a week she sat in the sweltering throne room, too close to the fire, with Gabek-Fen's less-than-encouraging direction to reach and take hold of the magic inside her. At first, it was like trying to wiggle her ears. She knew some people could do it, but she didn't know where to begin. She didn't seem to have the muscles for either ear wiggling or magic.

Finally, when both she and Gabek-Fen were starting to think she didn't have any magical abilities, she felt something stir within her. It was barely an inkling, a tickle in her subconscious, there one moment

22

and gone the next, but now she knew what it felt like. She found it again, coaxed it out from deep within her soul, and held it, warm and comforting in her mind. She willed it to do her bidding, and several small stones around her skipped across the floor. A pool of water formed at her feet as she coaxed droplets out of the dirt that was wedged between the crevices of slate. Magic coursed through her blood; she could feel it now. It spread through every inch of her body until it settled in her racing heart. From there, she could flex it like any other muscle.

Gabek-Fen patted her on the back and congratulated her as the pebbles on the ground levitated around her. Emya gazed around and smiled; she felt like a brand-new person. Not even the moans of distress from the Shadow could dampen her elation.

Her abilities increased exponentially every day. Sitting in front of the fire, she reached down inside herself with ease and concentrated on the magic of the flames before her. Azo nodded solemnly as the fire twisted into beautiful shapes. It wasn't a very useful manipulation, she couldn't move the fire from the wood and transfer it to another substance, but it was a good start. Azo had explained that keeping the fire burning without fuel was incredibly tricky.

"Very good," Azo said. "Lift that." He pointed at the throne.

Emya concentrated on the chair, lifting it into the air with some effort. It was heavy and the work of elevating it strained her as if she was lifting it with her arms and legs. She doubted she'd ever be able to lift much more than the throne, but the Kings insisted that eventually, her control of magic would exceed her physical limitations.

She put the chair down and Azo sat on it.

"You're making quick progress," he said. "How are

things going with the villagers?"

Emya grimaced. She had thought the combination of living with the Kings and learning magic would put her at risk of being lynched and that the kings would prudently keep her separated from the villagers. But shortly after she'd settled into her new life, the Kings instructed her to go into the village and bring back things they needed: food, water, grass for burning, and various herbs.

She hadn't expected to make it back alive the first time she was dispatched. Azo practically had to push her out the door. Instead of attempting to kill her, the villagers scrambled out of her way and refused to even look at her. When she was buying what she had been sent for, the merchant kept her eyes glued to the floor, refusing to take the coins Emya offered. She set the coins on a table and left. When she returned a week later, the coins were still on there, apparently untouched.

Emya reported this odd behavior to the Kings and, much to her horror, they instructed her to convince the villagers to speak to her and treat her as anyone else. At best, her neighbors tolerated her before she started learning magic; now their shunning her was the best reaction she could have hoped for. Nevertheless, the Kings insisted, so try she did. Nothing seemed to change the villagers' strange behavior.

"They're the same. They won't look at me or talk to me," she said one day after returning from the frosty silence of the village.

"Not that you want them to," Azo said matter-of-factly.

"Not really," Emya admitted.

His eyes narrowed as he looked at her silently. It was the same look that he had before he imparted profound wisdom that changed her perspective. A loud knock at the doors interrupted him before he could reveal anything.

"Enter," Azo called forcefully. The door eased open with the same apprehension Emya had the day she'd first been summoned. She allowed herself the small satisfaction that she no longer felt that way coming through those doors. Three villagers squeezed through: Amondo the baker; Lyla, a weaver; and Arn, a farmer and one of the more sensible residents.

Arn was a stout, busy man who'd merely shrugged when the Kings seized power. He had crops and cattle to care for and didn't have much time to worry about anything else. Everyone needed to eat, including the Kings, so he was left to himself. Emya almost liked him. He always had a friendly word and smile for her, but he was hardly ever around. If he was surprised to see her with the Kings his smile and nod in her direction didn't indicate it. Standing straight and tall, he appeared confident and relaxed. He acted as a spokesman and addressed the Kings on behalf of the other two.

"We're here on the matter of the annual trade festival," Arn said bluntly, speaking without the preamble that the other villagers felt necessary when they spoke to the Kings.

"What is that?" Azo asked, exasperated already by their presence.

"The closest village is almost a week's travel away. Few of us can spare the time to make the journey. Once a year we make time and take turns going to the other villages to trade. It's a big deal. Our first visitors will be arriving tonight."

Azo blinked several times and cocked his head as though Arn was speaking a foreign language.

"And you're just now asking my permission?" said Azo.

"Oh no, I'm not asking permission," Arn replied. "This is paramount to our survival as a community. I'm

25

just letting you know."

Amondo and Lyla looked to be on the verge of panic. Whatever bluntness they had expected from Arn was nowhere near as foolhardy as what he was delivering now.

Emya expected Azo to lose his temper and strike all three villagers down with a means most cruel and magic. To her endless astonishment, he did not.

"Very well," he replied to the farmer. "Have your festival. Go now. Don't bother us again."

Arn smiled and tipped his cap. As he turned to follow his companions out—they couldn't leave fast enough—he smiled at Emya again.

~~*~*~*~*

Alone once more, Emya resumed her practice while Azo left to find Gabek-Fen. She concentrated on the fire. The flames twisted, grew, and shrank with her will. One day she would be able to create fire with magic, so the Kings said.

A gentle shuffling of tired feet over slate disturbed her concentration as the Shadow appeared next to the fire. Despite the heat from the fire and the summer weather which turned the throne room into an oven, the young man always seemed to be cold. His pale, bony hands shook as he held them close to the flames. His greasy brown hair fell over his deathly white face as his bloodshot, golden eyes squinted in the light. He licked his dry, cracked lips.

She tried to ignore him and concentrate on her magic, but she couldn't help glancing at him out of the corner of her eye. He shivered violently, wrapped his arms around himself, and leaned closer toward the fire.

26

Without warning, his eyes rolled back in his head and he fell forward.

"Whoa," Emya jumped up to catch him before he could fall into the fire. His eyelids fluttered and opened when she grabbed him. He stared at her in confusion. She lowered him to the floor and felt his head. He was ice cold, corpse-like. Emya pulled her hand away, revolted.

"You're an undead monster!" she accused him. He shook his head weakly.

"I'm not dead," he mumbled. It was the first thing she'd ever heard him say. Moaning, he rolled onto his side and reached for her.

"Please," he whispered. "Water."

Emya stood up and backed away. She wasn't supposed to help him, but he might not leave her alone if she didn't. She dashed out to the well, tossed in the bucket, filled it halfway, and pulled it up quickly.

Inside, a water basin in the corner used for drinking water waited to be filled. The Kings became angry if she let it dry up, so she had to fill it anyway. After pouring in the water, she dipped a shallow bowl in the basin and brought it to the Shadow. He'd managed to get himself into a sitting position, but he shook so violently that she wasn't sure he would be able to hold the bowl.

As she approached he looked up at her with surprise and gratitude. And mistrust. He held out a trembling hand to take the bowl. Emya shook her head and gently pushed his hand down. She held the bowl to his lips and carefully tipped it, spilling the contents into his mouth and down his chin. Adjusting the pitch of the bowl, she held it while he slurped small sips.

His trembling slowed as the bowl emptied. When he was finished, he wiped his mouth with a steady hand. Rising to his feet without a word, he limped back to the corner. She hadn't noticed his labored gait before.

Watching his wretched, skinny form fall into a heap once more pierced her heart with pangs of sympathy.

She stood up and took a few hesitant steps towards him. The wooden doors burst open. Emya whirled around as the Kings sauntered in.

"You've practiced enough today," Gabek-Fen, the blunter of the two, said with a motion for her to leave.

Azo sat down on the throne, still absorbed in the object of power. "The festival starts tonight. You must go to it."

That was the last thing she wanted to do, but it wasn't a suggestion.

"Is there anything you would like me to do there?" she asked, hoping for some task she could complete and be on her way quickly.

"The villagers," he said, "keep working on them."

An impossible task.

Scurrying out of the throne room, she strode the short distance to the 'castle' in which the Kings had instructed her to live the day she left Kamala. She would have preferred her old house, which was still unoccupied, but was happy to have a place of her own. It wasn't much, but it allowed her privacy.

The castle had two rooms, a kitchen and a common room she used for sleeping and not much else. She lit a candle with a match from a little wooden box. It was one of the few items she'd rescued from her parents' house, and now it was nearly empty. After using her long-buried magic to twist and bend fire at will lighting candles the old-fashioned way was frustrating. She was anxious to progress to where she could light a fire with a snap of her fingers. Until then, the matches would have to do. At least with the festival she would be able to buy a new box and replenish her supply. The family that made them would almost certainly be there. Their neighboring village lay against a small forest of carefully cultivated trees, and beneath the soil were minerals that would burst into flame with not but a spark.

The annual festival had been her single reprieve each year. The visiting villagers had no idea she could use magic, and her people had no intention of revealing such a shameful secret. As a result, the visitors treated her like anyone else.

It wasn't likely that the visitors would notice the strange behavior neighbors displayed towards her now, as it wasn't much different from how they treated her during festivals past. Leaving her house that evening before sunset, she dragged her feet to the north border where the visitors were arriving and setting up for trade the next morning.

The market was already teeming with activity as the first arrivals set up their wares in the little mud-brick stalls that were used only once a year for the festival. The rest of the year, rain washed dirt into the stalls and weathered holes in the clay bricks. A harsh sun bleached the stalls, cracking and deteriorating the structures. But the weeks before the festival, the villagers dug out the dirt, patched the holes, cleaned the stalls, and lined the floor with fresh grass. Emya breathed in the smell of sweet straw and bitter churned soil. She closed her eyes for a moment, lost in the pleasant sensation. It wouldn't last long as the market gradually filled up with the smells of people, animals, and cooking food.

Excitement was palpable as Emya strolled through the market. No one took any notice of her as old friends reunited and new friends were made.

"Look who it is."

Emya turned to the familiar voice. Setting out a stack of little boxes was Emya's oldest family friend. Adrik, the match maker.

"Hello, Adrik. Have you found a match for me yet?"

Adrik laughed heartily, his long, shaggy gray hair falling into his wrinkled face.

"I don't have any young men for you, but I do have a gift."

He handed her a large matchbox, one that held more matches than her family could ever afford. She opened it, expecting some little trinket or interesting looking rock he'd found along the way. When she saw the contents, she snapped the box shut. It was filled with matches.

"I think you gave me the wrong box," she said, handing the gift back to him.

Confused, he took the box and opened it.

"No," he said, shutting it and holding it out to her. "This is the right one."

Emya didn't take it.

"I can't afford that," she said flatly.

"I know, that's why it's a gift." When she still wouldn't take it, he spoke again in a kinder tone. "I heard what happened to your parents. They were good people."

Emya nodded and took the box from him. The emotions she'd buried deep inside her threatened to overwhelm her. If she started crying now, she wasn't sure she'd ever stop.

"Thanks," she managed, her voice thick.

Leaving him to finish setting up, an excuse to get away, she wandered on through the market. She'd managed to avoid any kind of emotional display since the funeral and she wasn't going to start now. Outpourings of emotion drew attention, which had never been a good thing for Emya. Her parents knew this and taught her to push her feelings aside. Visitors at the festival smiled and waved at her if she got close enough, but her fellow villagers continued to pretend she was invisible. Mostly.

As she rounded the corner to the next row of stalls, she nearly collided with Kamala. Emya sidestepped the woman and attempted to skirt past her without notice, but Kamala turned from the other council members and caught sight of her before she could put the crowd between them.

"Emya!" she called sharply. It was the first time she'd spoken to Emya since she'd started learning magic.

"Yes?" Emya replied.

Kamala wasn't looking at her. Instead, she stared off over Emya's head, her eyes slightly glazed-over. It was how Emya's must have looked when she was listening to one of Kamala's lectures.

"Have you seen Arn?" Kamala asked, still looking over her.

"No."

"If you see him send him to me."

"Alright."

She then turned back to the councilors, who were looking at Kamala with concern. Emya hurried off before any of them decided to change their minds about talking to her.

Kamala hadn't actually ordered her to find Arn, and she knew Arn wouldn't care if Emya never delivered her message. He wasn't a fan of the current crop of councilors—and was fond of saying as much. Kamala was a particular irritant to him.

Distracted with preparing the festival, the villagers no longer scrambled to move out of Emya's way. She dodged between folks too distracted to notice her, ducking as villagers help two visitors maneuver a large crate of goods.

"'Scuse me there, sweetheart," a man said as he pushed past her. She looked up, expecting a visitor, but instead saw Harald, one of her toughest critics. Whatever she did, in his eyes, she did wrong. He must have been pretty busy not to notice her, but as she watched him wander off, he didn't seem to be in a hurry.

They were speaking to her. That was enough progress to report back to the Kings. She stopped and turned around, marching back to the throne room.

~~*~*~*~*

The throne room was empty and dark except for a thick candle and the Shadow it cast. He sat at the foot of the dais, an empty bowl and cup discarded nearby. The Kings didn't always remember to feed him.

"You're not supposed to be here," he whispered. Emya could barely hear him despite the utter silence.

"I'm also not supposed to talk to you. But here we are."

He answered with silence. His cheeks were gaunt, and his bright, fevered eyes cast down in defeat. She should have left him. She should have gone home and thought of him no more, but earlier, when she'd listened to his plea and given him water, she'd broken the rules and was now faced with a choice: tell the Kings about his speaking to her, ensuring they would not allow it to happen again, or sate her curiosity and continue their new arrangement in secret, bearing in mind the longer it when on, the worse it would be for them both if the Kings found out.

"Where are the Kings?" she asked. Of all the possible conversations, she picked the one topic that caused him the most pain. Sure enough, he squirmed uncomfortably, as though bitten by ants.

"Gone," he whispered. He hunched over and wrapped his arms around his stomach. "Did you do what they instructed?"

32

"Yes."

He shuddered. "And?"

Emya huffed and threw her arms up. All these weeks and all he wanted to talk about was the only topic ever discussed between her and the Kings? Though she was the one who'd brought them up.

"Everyone was busy," she said. "They didn't notice me. An improvement I'd say, but I imagine the Kings won't be satisfied with that."

"No," he agreed.

"What about you? Have you done whatever they need you for?"

"I don't do anything for them." He shuffled his feet under himself, leaned forward, and stood up, grimacing.

"Then why are you here?" she asked.

He hobbled toward his corner, ignoring the question.

"If I told you to run away, would you?" he asked, lowing himself onto the ground in the corner behind the thrones where the light of the fire was obscured. The darkness absorbed him into a denser, darker, shape in the void,

"No," she said. "Why should I?"

She'd thought about running away almost every day before the Kings arrived, but never could she muster the resolve to make the attempt. There were perils out there—wild animals, exposure, the elements—that only the security of a community could keep at bay. The Shadow had no idea. Even in his weakened state, he had the powerful Kings to protect him.

"Did anyone talk to you today?" he asked, disappointment in his tone.

"I told you everyone ignored me," she said and paused. Kamala talked to her, and not with scorn. "Kamala talked to me, but she was distracted by the festival."

"Don't you think it is odd that a whole village would decide not to talk to you?"

"No."

She hated how pathetic it sounded, but it was true.

"Have they really treated you that badly?" He sounded genuinely sympathetic but in comparison to what he'd gone through, it seemed petty. He had to be pointing that out, making fun of her stupid little problems.

"Yes, they have," she spat, venom in each word. He didn't know anything. She'd endured worse treatment every day since her parents died. Then the Kings took her in. Turning her back on him, she marched toward the door. the Shadow watched her go in silence.

She stomped into her house slamming the door hard behind her. The latch smashed into the frame and the door flew back open. Emya sighed heavily and examined it. Finding it wasn't broken, she closed the door carefully and latched it tight.

Leaning against the door, she sighed wearily. She longed for the comfort of her parents and the safety of their home more fervently than she had since their death. She'd always imagined living out her life there, taking care of them in their old age, and then enjoying a peaceful, isolated life when they were gone. Now she had her own house and independence from the villagers, but it wasn't peaceful.

She kicked off her shoes and crawled into bed. Things would have been different if they'd died when she was older. When she didn't need anyone to care for her. The village wouldn't have hated her so if they had seen her grow up a gentle, quiet member of the community. She would have never learned magic. Never hurt anyone. The Kings said her magic would kill her, but...

She drifted into a restless sleep, her dreams, usually fuzzy and unmemorable, were vivid that night, almost lifelike. In the hazy dreamscape of her village, she walked through the festival. It was an overcast and drizzly morning. The villagers chatted, bought and sold and traded with excitement and vigor. Yet something was wrong. A sense of dread filled Emya as she hurried through the crowds, trying to get away from some unknown danger. As she scurried along, she tried to warn people of the danger, but the villagers carried on, ignoring her.

It was gaining on her.

It would catch her any moment. She found the councilors chatting in the market square. Running past them, she slid under a cart. It was there in the square. The councilors didn't notice and suddenly they were gone. She scrambled out from under the cart and ran into the village. Suddenly she was at the well. The young man, the Shadow, leaned against the well. He turned and held out his hand.

"Run away," he said. She took his hand and abruptly was falling down the dark, endless well. She landed in the middle of the festival. It was night. Orange lights illuminated the sinister market. A sense of dread filled her, but also a sense of belonging. The villagers were dressed in terrifying costumes of black, shiny cloth and lace with swirling, unsettling, unreal patterns. As she followed the Shadow through the horrifying spectacle, she saw men fighting and stealing. Women wielded long, bloody knives. She sensed none of them would hurt her. She was safe from them. The Shadow led her to the edge of the village where she stopped.

"We must go," he urged.

She didn't want to go, she was safe in this chaotic, lawless village. Turning to look at the villagers, she noticed something new. Bright, shining, gold light covered their mouths and chained their hands and feet together. They glared at her with smoldering rage. The chains were there because of her, their looks said as much. She didn't put them there, but it was her fault. Suddenly the chains disappeared. A bone-chilling, inhuman shriek arose as the villagers charged towards her.

Chapter Three

Emya awoke sweating, shaking, and unable to move. As soon as she regained control of her muscles she pulled on her shoes and bounded out the door. The morning sun shined blindingly. Emya could barely see as she loped towards the throne room and burst in.

The Kings were absent. She hadn't considered if they'd returned, but she was glad they hadn't, as they would have prevented her from talking to the Shadow. He was lying on the ground in the corner, asleep until she marched up and stood over him, prodding him gently with her foot. He shifted uncomfortably and his eyes cracked open.

"Did the Kings use magic to make them stop talking to me?" she demanded, her voice high-pitched and wild. His eyes widened, surprised and afraid. He flinched as she took a step toward him, expecting to be hit.

"Yes," he breathed, cowering. He winced as she

stepped back.

She'd known it the whole time, deep down in her heart of hearts. Were the villagers aware? Magic could be used to influence people without their knowledge. If the villagers realized they'd been under some sort of enchantment she was sure to pay the price.

"I have to break the spell," she said more to herself, pacing away. Even if it meant the villagers would try to kill her. The Kings would have to protect her then.

"Yes," whispered the Shadow.

She could break the spell, somehow, or the Kings believed she could. Had she managed to break through the spell when Kamala talked to her? Or was that another effect of the spell?

But why? A little voice inside her whispered. Why did she have to free the villagers from a spell that was keeping them from tormenting her?

"How?" she demanded, turning back to him.

"I don't know. They want to see if you can figure it out yourself."

The doors swung open and the Kings sauntered in, each carrying a dead animal over their shoulders. The spotted red coats and distinct pointed ears and noses of valley leopards sagged pathetically. The rare cats roamed the steppe around the village, but almost never came close enough to be seen. She'd only heard them described by the few who'd ever seen them and survived.

"What are you doing here?" Gabek-Fen said as he tossed the carcass to the floor. There was no blood or wounds. It wasn't clear how they killed it, but its eyes were glazed in death. A pang of sadness struck her.

"I was looking for you," she lied. The Shadow crept slowly away from her as if they wouldn't notice.

"And you thought he might know where we were?"

Azo gestured to the boy.

"I was wondering what he was doing over here," she said, adding distaste to her tone. "He's always skulking around."

"Do not worry," Azo said softly. He seemed to think she was scared of the Shadow. "There is nothing in here for him to disturb, and he won't hurt you. He can't."

Emya nodded. She had no doubt in her mind that they had enchanted him to keep him from running away or fighting. Although it hadn't stopped him from talking to her.

"How did you fare last night?" Azo asked. "Were you able to make any progress?"

"Yes, Kamala talked to me a little."

"Good," Azo said with a smile. "You're doing very well."

"You must keep trying," Gabek-Fen said. "Go back to the festival."

Shaken and startled by their sudden appearance, she feared they would shortly surmise that she'd been conversing with the Shadow. Gabek-Fen still looked suspicious despite her explanation. To avoid further scrutiny, she marched out the doors. As soon as they clattered shut behind her, she ran all the way to the market.

The festival was in full swing. Stalls were filled with traders and the smell of roasting meat saturated the air. Excitement permeated the soul of the village. As she wandered through the market, she summoned magic from deep in her core. She stopped at a stall where two women were selling cloth that had been spun and woven from the little sheep they'd raised.

Emya ran her hand over the stacks of cloth. It was rough but well made. She observed the women. They weren't paying her any mind, too engrossed in unfolding and refolding the cloth.

"Hello?" Emya said, trying to catch their attention to no avail. Even if she'd waved her hands and jumped up and down, she doubted the women would have noticed. Whatever enchantment the Kings had placed on them was too powerful. She waved anyway and snapped in their faces, but they continued their folding, ignorant of her presence. A visitor appeared next to her. He greeted the women. They looked up and greeted him in return, though they continued their needless folding.

With a huff of frustration, Emya moved on through the crowded pathway in search of someone who might be easier to deal with. Arn, she decided. He'd acknowledged her before the festival, but after she was sure the Kings had already woven their enchantment, therefore he must not be under their spell. He would be somewhere in the market making sure everything was running smoothly.

Children ran past, laughing, and shoving each other. One smacked into her, nearly knocking her down. He didn't stop to apologize but instead ran around her to catch up with his friends.

She wandered through the maze of stalls, greeting people who passed her and waving at the vendors. The visitors always smiled and greeted her back, but the villagers ignored her. She reached out with her magic to rip off the spell, but it was like pulling stone set in mortar.

The villagers' behavior grew stranger. Several men and women wandered back and forth from two stalls without picking anything up or talking to the vendors. A pale, gaunt man was arguing over a basket of fruit, claiming it was rotten. The visiting vendor, an olive-skinned man with a bright orange beard, argued helplessly that the beautifully ripe fruit was not rotten. The villager held a piece, from which he had taken a bite, and Emya could see the cream-colored flesh inside was not rotten, yet he insisted it was.

"Excuse me," she said and tapped the pale man on the shoulder. The vendor looked at her pleadingly, but the villager ignored her. Emya concentrated, drawing up magic from deep within her core. It tingled in her fingertips and mouth, ready to go.

"Hey!" she barked. The man still ignored her. She tapped him again. "That's not rotten. Leave this man alone."

The villager turned to gawk at her. He cocked his head and his brow knit together. His piercing blue eyes were wide and wild as though he saw something terrible. Suddenly, he threw the basket at the vendor. His arms flew up to catch it, but the fruit hit him and fell to the floor. Emya started picking it up. The vendor stood, watching the villager leave, passing a piece of fruit irritably from hand to hand. Before the villager was out of range, he hurled the fruit at the man's head. It struck him so hard he stumbled and fell over. None of the passersby stopped to help or even took any notice at all. Instead, they merely walked around the body sprawled out in the path.

"Why did you do that?" Emya asked the vendor. He shrugged and tucked a lock of hair back into place behind his ear unconcernedly before returning the fruit to his stand.

The sound of many voices talking animatedly alerted her to a group moving down the lane. They kicked up dust as they went, coating their bleached-white lamb's wool robes with dark stains. Emya couldn't fathom why the councilors were wearing the ceremonial garments. Painstakingly made and treated with utmost care and due reverence, the robes were only worn on the most solemn occasions and ceremonies. They didn't belong to the councilors, though worn only by them. They were the village's most treasured possessions and they belonged to everyone.

She glanced around nervously. None of the villagers paid them any mind. She'd never cared for the robes the way the rest of the village had. She'd never thought of them as her own as everyone else did. If the Kings had cast a spell to elicit a strong response from her in order to drum up her powers, it wasn't going to work. Still, she had to try. The councilors would be furious when they realized what the enchantment made them do.

Pushing through the crowd, elbows and shoulders bumping and bruising her, she approached the councilors. Kamala, in the lead, chatted animatedly with Hai, whose face was twisted into laughter and cheer and almost unrecognizable. She'd never seen Hai so much as crack a smile. Emya felt something as she approached. It was overwhelming and pungent like a rotting carcass. It wasn't a smell, but it elicited the same feelings of revulsion and recoil as a large, dead animal. The rotten magic washing over her was enough to stir up the power within her and send it coursing through her body.

"Kamala," she called, marching up to the woman. She pushed past Emya without acknowledgment. Falling in step with Kamala, she tried again.

"Kamala!" This time she felt her magic break through the spell on Kamala. Finally, she turned and saw Emya. A huge, silly grin misshaped her features. Kamala threw her arm around Emya and pulled her along in a crushing hug. She smelled unwashed, reeking of sweat, dirt, and old food. Emya had never been this close to Kamala. Normally she kept herself out of arms reach from the volatile old councilor.

"Emya!" she said and giggled. "I've missed you. My old house is so quiet and cold without you to warm my heart."

Emya struggled against her grip. Kamala had always been strong, but this was an unnatural strength. Putrid magic washed over Emya in pulsating waves, beating against her own power. Straining her own magic, she willed it to find a weakness or some way to break the spell.

As though sensing the probing magic, Kamala pushed her away, still laughing and chatting, the enchantment not yet through with her. Emya sighed and watched them gambol through the market until they were out of sight. Then she turned and pushed through the throng before emerging onto the empty village streets. Slowing to a walk, she made her way to the throne room. Something was terribly wrong; the spell had mutated into something horrible and dangerous. The Kings had to lift the spell before the village descended into madness.

She stumbled to a stop at the village square. Six couples danced a clumsy, drunken waltz while several onlookers clapped out a rhythm that did not match the steps. From behind, someone suddenly grabbed her hand and pulled her into the dance.

"No, let me go!" she cried.

She pulled away and twisted her arm, but the grip was strong as Kamala's had been. Whirling her around, he began to waltz and Emya gaped at the familiar face.

"Adrik what are you doing? Let me go!" She planted her feet, forcing him to dance awkwardly in place. She peered into his face pleadingly, but he was blind to her. His eyes glazed-over and his expression blank except for a slight twitch in one eye. She stomped with all her might on his foot and was rewarded with a grunt of pain and slackened grip, enough for her to break away. Without a backward glance, she made a mad dash for the council chamber.

Slamming the door shut behind her, she drew

the heavy iron bolt across the doors. Still trembling, heart pounding, she turned then gasped. At the foot of the dais, Gabek-Fen and Azo crouched. The Kings were mumbling and tracing symbols on the stone. The Shadow slouched between them, white as snow and trembling violently. Symbols tattooed in searing light on his bare chest, arms, and face oozed a clear fluid. The Kings dipped their fingers in the pool around him, drawing symbols with it on the floor. At their touch, the clear ooze shimmered and turned black. Completely engrossed in their work, neither of the Kings noticed Emya's arrival.

With great effort, the Shadow raised his head. His eyes, sunken in their sockets, filled with pain and fear. His colorless lips pleaded silently. Turned to stone, Emya looked on in horror.

After several agonizing minutes, the Kings finished drawing the symbols and placed their hands in the liquid pooling around the Shadow, absorbing it. The Shadow screamed a cry of such intense agony that it stirred Emya's most raw instincts and woke something inside her—something so terrified that it thrashed and roared to be let loose, to take its vengeance.

When the pool dried up the symbols disappeared. The Kings stood up, ignoring the Shadow, who fell onto his back, unmoving.

"He won't die," Azo said, seeing Emya's horrified expression. "His magic keeps him alive as long as he is not mortally wounded. As does yours."

"What did you do to him?" her voice barely louder than a breath. As the ritual ended, the feelings of horror and terror began to fade within her and whatever had been awoken inside her settled back into her subconscious. She did not have time to analyze it, but instinctively knew that it was different than anything she'd ever felt.

"We took his magic," Gabek-Fen said gruffly, as he did when he thought she was asking too many personal questions.

"Fen," Azo said warningly. He turned to Emya with a placating expression. "We wanted to wait to show you until you had developed your skills more. That way you would have understood. Now, I suppose we must explain ourselves."

He picked up something off the floor beside the shadow. It was the object of power and it had turned onyx black.

"As I said before, this object will draw power from you and, if you have the strength, direct it for you. That property has other uses as well, this one here." He kicked the Shadow hard in the ribs. He whimpered, too weak to drag himself away. "He was a very powerful natural mage, and he used his power to destroy other mages. We drain him of his power and direct it to ourselves. He is only left with enough to live on and nothing more until his powers regenerate. Unfortunately, magic isn't meant to be taken from a person like him. Even when using an object such as this, much of it is lost, drained into the world. We split what we are able to get between ourselves. It is enough to allow us modest power."

Their power might have been modest but their egos sure weren't. She'd never imagined they hadn't been born with magic as she had. Now she knew what purpose the Shadow served. A purpose dark and dreadful. She knew why he asked her if she would leave. Why hadn't he told her what the Kings were doing to him in order to make her leave? Was he afraid she would try to take his magic too? This was why they wanted her. This was why they took her in, nurtured and trained her, to take his place, to have two sources of power.

Perhaps not, a small, desperate voice said within her, perhaps the Shadow was enough. Perhaps they would keep her as they said, their student, and one day their equal. She could do much more for them as an ally than a prisoner.

"How is your progress with the village?" Azo asked, changing the subject. He sat down on his throne, a teacher evaluating his student. Emya couldn't keep her gaze from the Shadow, pale and trembling, closer to death than she'd ever seen him.

"Emya," Gabek growled. He took her chin in his hand and forced her gaze up to his. "Answer my brother."

Emya turned to Azo, remembering why she'd come in the first place.

"It's getting worse," she said. "Kamala talked to me, but I don't think she was in her right mind. Everyone is acting strangely. Please, you have to take the spell off."

Azo leaned forward in his chair, a vicious smile framed his predatory gaze. She took a step back instinctively, fighting off an overwhelming urge to flee the throne room and the village beyond it. Gabek-Fen paced behind her, blocking her escape.

"Yes, I agree," Azo said. "The spell has begun to run rampant. That's a danger with magic. It is so easy to lose control, especially with long term use." He held up the object and examined it admiringly.

"Objects like this allow us to control magic more easily, though not as well as it would if we had our own magic." He held it out to her. "You have the power to break the spell, but not on your own. This will direct and amplify your powers. Use it."

As Emya took the object with shaking hands, she glanced at the Shadow. He'd pulled himself into a sitting position and watched with wide, fearful eyes. Her gaze met his for a moment. He shook his head ever so slightly, but it was too late. The moment the object contacted her skin, she felt it take hold of the power deep inside her. Panic struck her. The object fell from her hands, thumping solidly on the floor, but she could still feel it, a connection, as though a thin, invisible and unbreakable string tethered her to it.

She looked up at Azo. He smiled that wicked, conniving smile.

"Sorry," she said, stooping to pick up the object. His hand beat hers to it, scooping it off the floor. He held it aloft, admiring it.

"Throwing it at the wall as hard as you can would not break it." He held it out to her once more. She took it, warm in her hands. Nothing happened.

"What do I do?" she asked.

"What we trained you to do. It will work," Azo assured her.

"You said it would consume my power if I don't know how to control it."

"Well," Azo said, leaning back on his throne, "we'll find out, won't we?"

She glanced at Gabek-Fen. He watched, a smile playing on his brutish features. She peeked at the Shadow. He was curled up on the floor, his face hidden in his arms except for his peering eyes, dull with exhaustion.

Turning her attention to the object, she took a deep breath and closed her eyes. When she reached down, deep down, she fell, losing all control, but gained more power than she ever imagined. She opened her eyes and the room was dark except for the once roaring fire's muted light, like a candle in an abyss. She grasped the power inside her and focused on her desire to break the enchantment.

She could see it, the enchantment. It looked like a shimmering black chain of tiny orbs that burst and reformed, as it snaked through an outline of the village. It filled her with dread, but she knew she could break it. With a thought, she cut through the chain. The orbs flew apart and burst. Relaxing, she released her magic.

Pain blossomed in her chest, leaving her gasping. It felt as though her heart was being sucked into the object. Panicking, she struggled to regain control of her magic. The flow to the object slowed and stopped. The object tugged at the magic, but she held on. Her knees buckled under her. After several grueling minutes, the object relinquished, though she could feel its attachment lingering. Slowly, she relaxed. When the object didn't resume its tug of war she looked up at the Kings, who were watching her intently. Azo nodded in satisfaction.

"You have succeeded," he said. "We will begin your training in earnest tomorrow. You will learn how to use the object and how to perform enchantment beyond your imagination, but we must leave this place."

"Leave the village?" she murmured. It was her deepest desire and greatest fear to leave her home, the place that had caused her so much pain. She'd imagined leaving so many times, whisked away by the Kings, with whom she thought she would be safe. No longer. They would use the object to take her magic as sure as they would take the Shadow's.

"You must get ready to leave," Azo said. "Go home now."

Emya turned and darted through the doors. She rushed to her house, avoiding the festival that was spilling into the rest of the village. She had broken the spell, why were they still acting like mad people? As she closed the door and fell into bed, she began to shake and sob as the weight of what had transpired fell over her.

The young man, the Shadow, she'd been so cruel to him. She'd believed the Kings when they told her that he was nothing, worthless, not worth her time. The whole time they'd been sucking away his magic, leaving him in the most pitiable state. She'd gone along with it. Never did she question it, instead she believed herself different. He'd even tried to warn her, but now it was too late.

No. She jumped out of bed with her mind racing and heart pounding. She dashed out the door. Her feet carried her through the village, picking a path of their own. Her mind caught up as she ran through the festival, dodging reveling villagers until she came to the road that the visitors had arrived on. It would take her straight on to the next village. She ran, stumbling along with the cracked and loose paving until it gave way to a dusty dirt path.

She slowed to a walk, sucking in breath. The village was still visible, but only barely—a small blotch in the distance. She turned back and considered the valley. It was a few hours before nightfall, and hopefully, nothing roaming the grasslands would be interested in eating her.

It had been some time since she'd thought about her parents when they were alive. She'd driven their memory from her mind when it began to interfere with her concentration as Azo instructed her. He probably had other reasons for wanting her to forget her parents. It was another way to isolate her from her old life, to make her more like the Shadow. Sorrow, anger, and fear prickled in her eyes; tears blurred her vision. No, that wasn't it. A dizzy faintness filled her head. She stumbled a few steps and collapsed.

Chapter Four

Heat seared her face first before spreading down her body. Light burned through her eyelids. The loud click and pop of burning grass and wood, along with the intense heat, suggested she was next to a fire. All strength had left her. She lacked even the energy to open her eyes, let alone move away from the licking flames. There was only one place in the village that had a wood fire. With tremendous effort, she pried her eyes open. Bright blurry light forced her to close them again, but she was indeed in the throne room. Gradually she recalled what happened and could guess how she'd been returned, though why she had passed out so suddenly was not immediately clear. The Kings must have somehow figured out what she was doing and put a spell on her.

After a few minutes, strength trickled through her, and with some effort, she turned away from the heat. Cool air bathed her face and encouraged her to open her eyes again. She was not alone. Through blurry vision, she could discern the scrawny, wasted figure sitting beside her. She blinked several times and he came into focus.

The Shadow watched her dully, his expression resigned and hopeless. She hadn't realized there was some hope in him before, but now it was gone. At least some color had returned to his cheeks and thin, cracked lips, though it did little to improve his corpse-like countenance.

"You tried to run, didn't you?" he said, his voice barely a hoarse whisper.

"Yes," she breathed.

"It won't let you. The object." He shuddered. "When they leave and take it with them, I pass out too."

That explained why he often seemed to be asleep while the Kings were away hunting. When the Kings were in the room he was always awake. She saw out of the corner of her eye the way his bright, fearful gaze followed their every move. When he'd been able to talk to her while the Kings were away, they must have been nearby. Which meant they were not far now.

"They have no power of their own," he continued. "Never have. They went to a forbidden place where powerful objects are hidden. Most die before ever finding one, but the Kings are cunning and strong. They found an object that could give them the power they desired."

He pushed himself closer and leaned toward her, an effort that drained the little color in his face.

"When I die, they will get their power from you," he said. "Don't believe me? You soon will."

She believed him. Despite everything the Kings had ever told her, the tether which connected her to the object which she could sense as keenly as a limb attached to her magic, was proof enough of their true intentions.

The Shadow had been very sick when they arrived. They must have known he didn't have much time left. Must have been searching. Their appearance in the village was part of the search for a replacement.

"Did they know I had magic?" she asked in a low, scared voice. "Did they come here because of me?"

"I don't know," he said. "They don't tell me anything, nor am I usually able to listen when they talk."

Emya closed her eyes and took a deep breath to calm the panic rising in her. The villagers had been right about her all along. Whether she used it or not, her magic had caused everyone to suffer. Even if the Kings hadn't come for her intentionally, she was one of the reasons they stayed.

"You wanted to know if I would leave if you asked me to before," she said. Her strength had returned enough to sit up. "I wish I had. It's too late now, I suppose."

"It's not too late," he murmured looking up at her through his lashes. The heavy wooden doors flew open. In thundered the Kings, arguing savagely. When Gabek-Fen caught sight of Emya and the Shadow, he stomped over to them, roaring.

"We told you not to talk to her!" He hauled up the wretched young man and hurled him across the room. Slamming against the wall, he fell to the floor with a sickening thump and did not stir. Gabek-Fen rounded on Emya.

"Next time it'll be you!"

He stalked away and threw himself onto a throne. Azo crouched next to her, smiling the gentle smile she used to trust. It was unsettling how she could detect no deceit in his features.

"My poor little Emya," he said, reaching out and stroking her hair. She flinched away but he ignored it, gently combing through her knotted locks.

"You wandered too far from us. You must stay in the village now until your training is complete. If you stray too far from the object for too long you will die. You don't want that to happen, do you?"

She shook her head. He patted her affectionately on her arm and she fought the urge to cringe away. She needed them to think she had learned her lesson, at least until she had a plan. A commotion outside distracted the Kings. A cacophony of laughing and shouting advanced on the throne room. Azo stood up, regarding the door with a frown.

"I told you it wouldn't work," growled Gabek-Fen.

"We will try again," Azo said diplomatically.

He marched out the door, Gabek-Fen grumbling behind him. "It won't work I tell you."

The doors slammed shut behind them. Emya waited a few moments before standing up. With considerable effort, she shuffled over to the Shadow. She knelt next to him and placed her hand on his chest to feel for a heartbeat. A weak thump pulsed, but she needn't have checked. The Shadow placed his hand lightly over hers. A confusing but pleasant feeling filled her own chest. Before she could better examine it, the Shadow's eyes fluttered open.

"Are you badly hurt?" she asked gently.

"I don't think so," he said. "Not any worse than I was before."

She helped him sit up and propped him against the wall.

"You said it's not too late," Emya said. "We can still leave."

"I said it wasn't too late for you to leave. I'm too weak."

Casting her gaze down, filled with anger and guilt, Emya silently scolded herself. If she'd realized sooner what now seemed so obvious, she might have saved him, but she'd been blinded by her grief and helplessness. She let her emotions consume her, leaving no room for anyone else. This didn't make the Shadow's predicament her fault by any means, but she'd been complicit, even if she had little choice.

"I can't go alone," she said. "I was being rash when I ran away before. I didn't bring anything with me. I don't know how long I would have lasted."

That coaxed out of him a smile and a small laugh.

"Not long I'm afraid," he said.

"You've traveled though, and you know magic—better than I do, I'll bet. I need you."

The Shadow considered this, frowning. Through his exhaustion, a light of hope kindled in his eyes.

"Alright," he said after a few moments. "I will go with you. If we can make it to my people, they might be able to save me. If they can't, at least you will be safe with them."

Emya sighed with relief then took a deep, steadying breath as she resolved herself to do what she knew she must.

"I have to get the object from them, don't I?" she said.

"Yes."

A near-impossible task, as the Kings never let it out of their sight.

"I can't take it from them by force. I doubt I could trick them into giving it to me..." she mused.

"In my time connected with the object I've learned a little about it." He was interrupted by a coughing fit. Emya waited for it to pass. She imagined she wouldn't like what he had to tell her, but it would be their only chance.

"By the time I realized how I could use that knowledge to my advantage," he went on after a moment of slow, deep breathing, "I was too weak. From what I've discerned, the object wants to take power from the mage it connects with. It is not meant to give that power to someone without magic. I can only guess, but I think it is meant to be used to give that power to another mage. Regardless, I believe that the mage that the object is connected to has more control over the object that someone who is not. Since the Kings have no magic of their own, they can never be connected to it. I believe you could summon the object away from them, from a distance too."

"As long as I'm close enough to the object that I don't pass out," Emya said. He nodded.

Emya got to her feet, a plan already forming. She would need to prepare properly first.

"We can go to the edge of the village," she said. "But I don't know how to summon the object."

The Shadow, now visibly aggravated, huffed. Though it was not at her, she realized.

"If you were properly trained in the ancient language it would be so simple," said the Shadow.

"A magic language?" She'd heard of spells being cast with magic words, some words were even banned in the village because they were supposed to be magic, though she'd heard them uttered many times under angry or frustrated breath.

"Yes," he said. "It was created specifically for magic."

"Then teach me what I have to say!"

"It's not that simple, but we have no other choice. I will try to tell you what to say, but not until we are ready. Now go, prepare quickly, and return."

They didn't know where the Kings were or when they would return. Speed was critical. Emya ran to her house, and when she arrived, she threw her clothes, the little food she had, and matches into a bag. Almost as an afterthought, she grabbed her old knife, placing carefully on top of the other items so it was easily accessible.

She quickly returned to the throne room and found that the Kings were still absent. Near the door stood the Shadow, pale and sickly, but resolved. He took an unsteady step towards her. She hurried to his side and put his arm around her shoulders. She'd never realized how much taller he was until she was standing next to him. He had at least a head and a half on her.

The sun had set they found when they peeked out the door. There was no moonlight in the silent village square. A tingling tinge of magic rippled over them. The Shadow straightened up and looked around sharply.

"They've conjured a barrier," he said softly. "It keeps the villagers away."

"Will it let us through?"

"I think so," he said after a moment. "But it might not let us back in."

Emya nodded. Returning was of no consequence to her, as she had no intention of ever setting foot in the throne room again.

Fresh air and the prospect of freedom seemed to spur him forward as she helped him along through the square. As they passed through the barrier, the silence broke into the sounds of laughing and screaming. The revelry seemed to be contained to the festival grounds as they walked through the deserted streets. When they neared the market the Shadow froze, forcing her to stop.

"What is it?" she asked.

"You said the Kings put a spell on the villagers?" he murmured

"Yes, but I used the object to break it. Did they put another one on them?"

He shook his head.

"This is no magic of the Kings or the object. We

must go," he said urgently.

She adjusted her hold on him to support him more securely. Together they continued on through the village, he hobbled along beside her, sweaty and pale. They stopped when they arrived at the festival.

The stalls were abandoned, some destroyed, and their contents scattered in the streets. Lamps cast their dimmed yellow light over the ground where the villagers lounged, laughing, crying, and screeching in delight. A few wandered aimlessly, swaying drunkenly and tripping over debris, as it had been in her nightmare.

Emya and the Shadow avoided stepping on villagers by moving carefully over and around them, no easy task as the villagers would suddenly roll or flop to one side or another as if trying to get under their feet. Unless Emya and the Shadow drew near, the villagers would take no notice of them.

The Shadow wasn't heavy, diminished as he was, but still she struggled to hold him as he stumbled over the uneven path. A pair of villagers danced drunkenly past, bumping into him, nearly knocking them over.

"We're almost there," she whispered. The last few stalls were before them and Emya could see the road. Between the last two booths, someone stumbled out into their path. Emya stopped and backed away. Kamala swayed from side to side, tottering towards them, her face twisted in rage.

"You did this!" she screamed, unhinged. "You brought this curse upon us!"

Emya tried to push the Shadow out of the way and duck as Kamala swung at her. The punch missed her but struck the Shadow so hard that he tumbled from her grip and fell into the dirt.

Kamala brushed past Emya, kicking the shadow, screaming incoherently. Grabbing the woman by her dress, Emya hauled her away.

The spell gave Kamala strength beyond that of the Kings. It took all Emya's might to keep the flailing woman at bay, her grasp slipping. Emya summoned her magic and willed the woman to sleep. She hadn't expected it to work, not with so much of her concentration focused on restraining Kamala, but to her intense relief, Kamala suddenly slumped to the ground, snoring gently. Emya had no time to analyze her sudden magical prowess. No doubt it was related to the object or the magic saturating the festival. She hurried over to where the Shadow was still curled in the dirt.

"You have to get up." He flinched when she grabbed him by the arm, curling in tighter. "We have to keep going," she urged.

He wouldn't budge and Emya couldn't carry him. She knelt next to him. "It's okay," she said gently, "no one's going to hurt you anymore, but you have to get up."

After a moment, his eyes blinked open and he relaxed enough to let Emya help him sit up. Gingerly touching the back of his head, he winced and examined the blood that stained his fingers.

"She's strong," he murmured dimly, wiping the blood on his shirt. Emya helped him to his feet and on they stumbled out of the market and onto the road.

They stopped. Without knowing where the object was, they risked passing out again if they went too far— assuming the Kings were still in the village. It was time to summon the object, but Emya faltered. Her hastily constructed plan had several holes in it. Assuming the Shadow knew where to go from there, she had no idea what lay between them and their first destination, the neighboring village. More concerning were the Kings. Even if she managed to summon the object from them, it was only a matter of time before they noticed, she, the Shadow, and the object were all gone.

The Shadow broke out in another coughing fit.

He clung to her, convulsing violently, spewing flecks of blood. This was his only chance and likely hers as well. She would have more time as they slowly drained the magic from her, but there was no guarantee she would ever have another chance to escape.

"Alright," she said. "What do I have to do?"

"Call the object in the ancient tongue. You have to picture it in your head when you call."

He said the words slowly and clearly. They weren't long or hard to pronounce. She called the magic inside her said the words out loud while picturing the object in her head, willing it to leave the Kings and come to her. Nothing happened.

"Glaiuad tugum erotude."

"It didn't work," the Shadow said flatly. "You're too inexperienced"

"Well you do it then," Emya said desperately.

"I don't have the strength. Try again."

Emya said the words once more. Again and again she said the words. She'd worried so much about what they would do when she got the object that she hadn't considered what failing to do so meant. She hadn't pictured walking back through the village to the throne room, praying the Kings hadn't noticed. Now she was paralyzed with fear at the realization. They couldn't go back. They were so close to being free.

"Running away?" A cool, familiar voice said.

Azo appeared before them from the shadows of the festival.

Chapter Five

Enormous, deadly, and disturbingly relaxed, Azo regarded Emya and the Shadow as though they were naughty children. Attached to his waist was the pouch containing the object, almost within her reach. She could take it by force or cunning, but he would kill her as soon as she moved. The Shadow whimpered in fear, clutching her arm so tightly it hurt.

Azo pulled the object from the pouch and held it before them, a dim glow fluoresced from it. A sign of some new use he'd found for it no doubt.

"I knew you were trying to summon it the moment you said the words," Azo said softly, deadly. "You may be connected to the object, but I alone control it. I told you not to talk to the boy and now he's tried to teach you the ancient language." Azo shook his head with a derisive laugh. "Superstitious nonsense. Magic comes from inside you. That language only makes you weak. He's trying to control you. I can make you powerful. I will teach you as I promised if you don't make me kill you."

"You're lying," Emya said, stalling. The object glowed brighter, though Azo didn't seem to notice. The Shadow slumped against her, evidently too weak to hold himself up any longer. "You're going to take my magic just like you took his."

Azo shook his head again with a bitter smile.

"He hasn't told you the whole story. If you knew, you'd believe that I do not wish to take your magic."

"I don't think I would," she said, the object was as bright as a flame and humming like a violin now. Emya knew if she called it now it would come to her, there was nothing Azo could do to prevent it. He may have been its master once before, but not anymore. The problem was, what to do when she had it?

Azo sighed. "I do not want to take your magic, but if you won't cooperate, I will be forced to do so."

His hand went to the pouch. Emya knew, though she didn't know how, if he put the object away that it would be out of her reach. As his fingers brushed the pouch, Emya shouted the words. The object appeared in her hand. She gripped it.

The world blinked and Azo was gone. Emya looked around. The village was gone too, replaced by tree trunks and not much else.

"Where are we?" she breathed.

The Shadow clutched her arm, still trembling and pale but on his feet. He let go, staggered to a wide tree trunk, and rested against it.

"This is a forest near my home," he said. "The object transported us here. We are safe for now."

Emya, still dazed, sat next to him. She was burning with questions, most of which she could not put into words. She decided to begin with the simplest.

"How?" she asked.

61

"As soon as you had the object," he said, "I knew I could use it to transport us. I thought it might kill me, but evidently not."

Emya frowned.

"I knew I could take it," she said. "It was glowing. I thought that meant something."

The Shadow nodded, rubbing his eyes with both shaking hands.

"I saw the glowing too, but I don't think Azo could see it," he said.

"I don't understand. Was it our connection? How was it telling us what to do?"

"I don't know," he said. "I don't know exactly how it works."

Exhausted, Emya reclined against the large trunk and looked around. She hadn't seen a forest since she was very little. The trees were enormous with reddish-brown trunks stretching into a dense canopy of dark green foliage. The ground below was covered in thick moss. Patches of shrubs dotted the less shaded areas. A small, brown animal with a long fluffy tail darted from the trunk of a tree and began to dig.

After a while, Emya realized she was still holding the object. It had turned a light gray color. If she hadn't known better, she would have thought it was nothing but a rock.

"What is this called?" she asked.

Slumped against the tree, eyes shut, the Shadow seemed to have fallen asleep.

"It doesn't have a name," he said wearily. "It never needed one."

She didn't care to call it *the object*, but it needed a suitable name.

"We'll call it 'the companion,'" she said, "since we can't leave it behind."

The shadow chuckled.

"An accurate description."

While they were on the topic, Emya asked, "What is your name?"

"Felix." He opened his eyes in surprise.

She looked at the ground, too embarrassed to meet his gaze.

"I should have asked sooner."

"It's alright. Azo and Fen never asked, even after three years." Clutching his chest, a fit of coughing overcame him.

"Where can we find help?" Emya asked.

"A village," he said when the fit subsided. "In the Valley of Tritium Mountain." He leaned forward with a great shuddering sigh. Emya frowned. If he died out in the middle of nowhere, she would likely perish soon after.

"Can you walk?" she asked anxiously.

"I don't think so," he said, leaning back up against the tree. "We can rest here for the night. It will be safe enough."

He instructed Emya to collect wood for a fire. She did so, finding plenty of thin branches scattered nearby. She did not dare wander out of sight from him. After stacking the branches, she rummaged through her pack for matches. Felix murmured something; the branches caught fire. He smiled weakly.

"They kept me from doing magic. It seems their hold over me is broken," he said.

She tended the fire, adding branches until it was sufficiently large enough to last several hours, then curled up on the ground. Energy spent, Emya closed her eyes, too tired to keep watch. There wasn't much either one of them could do if something found them asleep and vulnerable, but her mind wouldn't let her sleep. Her imagination swirled with images of the furious Kings using magic to locate them and transporting to the forest just as they had. Something crunched the branches nearby. She sat up, peering around wildly. It moved between the trees; four-legs and huge antlers passed by. It stopped and sniffed the ground, then kept going.

Emya let out a breath. A deer. Larger than the little creatures that roamed the tall grasses around her village, but nothing dangerous as long as she didn't bother it. She settled down once more, turning onto her side she saw the Shadow—Felix—was awake.

"It was just a deer," she whispered.

"I know," he said. "I could hear it. Did it frighten you?"

"I thought it was the Kings. I thought they transported here."

Felix's eyes fluttered shut.

"They can't," he murmured. "It's too difficult for them."

"Why?" she asked, momentarily distracted from her exhaustion and fear. She never thought there was any magic the Kings were not capable of.

"They aren't mages and have no natural magic. That limits their abilities considerably."

She could not imagine the Kings being unable to do any kind of magic. They'd awed her with displays of immense power, creating large fires, giving themselves impossible strength, levitating objects. Other kinds of magic were inconceivable to her. She turned to Felix to ask but stopped. Blank faced and peaceful, he'd fallen into sleep. Settling down again Emya fell into restless sleep too.

Light shone dimly through the canopy when she woke. Sore despite the spongy moss carpet, she sat up slowly. Felix was curled up, snoring gently. At least he was still alive. Though the forest was quiet and peaceful, an eerie essence permeated the air. A gentle breeze swept through the trunks, colder than it ought to have been. Shivering, she stood up and walked around the great red trunk they were camped under. Nothing moved between the trees, no deer, or any other creature, but she could not shake the feeling that something was nearby.

"Emya?" Felix called weakly. She scampered back around the tree.

Felix was sitting up, looking worse than he had the night before. It didn't seem possible that he would be able to make it through the forest.

"Are you feeling any better?" she asked, sitting cross-legged beside him and rummaging through her pack.

"A little less tired," he said, "but worse than I would feel if I hadn't used the companion I think."

She had expected a long journey and had packed plenty of food. She handed him a hard roll, dried fruit, and some water. He ate it quickly.

"Don't make yourself sick," she said.

"They used to take my food away before I finished," he said softly. "I'm used to eating fast."

Emya's heart ached.

"You don't have to eat fast now," she said. "Take your time."

"Actually," he said around a mouth full, "I think we'd do better to get going as quickly as possible."

When they finished eating a few minutes later, Felix got shakily to his feet. How far he would be able to walk was uncertain, but Emya took him by the arm and let him lean on her as they set off.

The trees were magnificent and Emya had a hard time taking her eyes off them. Felix directed her along a winding path through the trees and she became sure they were going in circles. Twice they climbed a steep slope and down a shallow incline, both of which looked and felt identical.

"Are you sure we're going the right way?" she asked tentatively.

"Yes," he said, a little out of breath. "I've been through these woods many times, but we must hurry. We're being followed."

Emya increased their pace, pushing Felix's endurance as much as she dared. No sound but their footfall permeated the silence, but out of the corner of her eye shadows flickered with ominous presence. For several hours they walked; Felix held up until noon. His steps slowed while his stumbling increased. They sat to rest beneath a large redwood with a sizable hole gouged out of the trunk. Emya kept glancing up at it, worried about what sort of creature might call it home, until Felix assured her it was empty.

"How do you know?"

"Same way I know we're being hunted. Magic, to detect the presence of creatures. We must move on quickly."

Felix caught his breath while Emya took out some lunch. They ate silently until Emya could stand it no longer.

"How much further?" she asked. It was the question most burning in her heart. She did not want to badger him while he concentrated on walking.

"We should reach the valley by nightfall," he said.

"Good. This place gives me such a sense of unease."

Felix nodded solemnly.

"It used to be a happier place, long ago. Before a raging storm of raw magic stripped it of its nature."

At the quizzical look from Emya he went on.

"There was a battle in this forest among mages. It damaged the trees irrevocably and I'm afraid much of the magic still lingers here."

"Is it safe? The magic I mean," she asked, wondering

66

what could have possessed him to bring them there.

"We are protected by our powers. Any person without magic would go insane or worse. Few wander in. Only those of immense courage and strength could survive without magic."

"You said there is something in here though."

"Yes," he said gravely. "A creature of magic. It found us some time last night, I think."

"The deer?"

"No that was just an animal. They come in here sometimes. Deer don't seem to be affected by raw magic. We should go," he added sharply.

With Emya's help, he got to his feet and they started off. Felix set the pace. When the sun began to set, the green light dimmed to a shadowy gray. As the shadows grew so did her sense of foreboding. The forest came to life with flickering shadows. A shimmer between trunks, a flash in the foliage, a patch of darkness that disappeared when she tried to look at it properly. Felix quickened their steps.

As the sun set and the woods succumbed to darkness, something in the canopy let out a soul-rattling cry. Emya looked up to see the creature leaping between the lower branches of the canopy, entirely silent. Large leathery wings stretched out as it glided through the air, great clawed talons grasping limbs as thick as her thigh. It flew ahead of them, watching and waiting. Felix gripped her arm tightly and pulled her into a fast trot.

"It's a Faolgal. A demon bird," he whispered. "Just a little further—hurry!"

Felix broke into a run, pulling Emya along with an energy only mortal peril could summon. As they passed underneath, it dived, striking Emya. Its talons dug into her shoulder. Crying out in agony, she grabbed at its claws as it beat its leathery wings and lifted her into the air. Felix wrapped his arms around her, hauling her and the creature to the ground. Releasing her, it flew up and Emya collapsed in Felix's arms. He set her on her feet and pulled her into a run.

The Faolgal circled around and dived. They ducked but it slashed their heads with its talons. Its sharp, long beak bit into Felix, and he howled in pain and collapsed. Emya grabbed her pack and swung, striking the bird so hard it flew ten feet into a tree trunk.

It fell into a heap on the ground, but quick as lightning it lurched to its feet and let out a horrible, gurgling scream. With its wings spread to their full length, it was longer than any man. Agitated, it leaped at them. Emya stood frozen, still clutching Felix's arm as death descended on her.

There was a sickening thump.

The Faolgal crumpled to the ground. A big knife embedded in its back up to the hilt. Behind it stood a man, silhouetted in the night.

~~*~*~*~*

He took five long strides to meet them, kneeling next to Felix.

"Not dead," he said in a soft voice just above a whisper.

"You were almost out too," he added, hefting Felix into his arms. He loped off, not waiting to see if Emya would follow. More afraid of losing Felix than this stranger, Emya scampered after him.

"Who are you?" she asked, jogging to keep up with his long stride.

"Artyem. I am one of the Guard of Civim," he said as though that was reason enough to trust him.

"The what?"

"The Citadel," he said. "I thought Felix would have told you."

He knew Felix; maybe she could trust him.

"He hasn't told me much. He's sick."

"I can see that," he said. "Stay close, we're nearly there."

Sure enough, as they summited a particularly steep slope—one that Emya had to crawl near the top for fear of slipping—the tree line appeared. Beyond, lights twinkled among houses, silhouetted in the last rays of the setting sun. Artyem did not stop to admire the charming scene, nor to let her catch her breath, instead striding with urgent haste toward the village.

When they arrived it was fully dark, but villagers still wandered the streets under tall lamps and light streaming from windows. The villagers smiled pleasantly as they passed by with a careless expression, not unlike the way her neighbors had looked before they utterly lost their minds. She stuck close on Artyem's heels. The houses were unlike those in her village. Constructed out of wood and with windows that were impossibly clear, Emya could see the inhabitants inside laughing and talking. She looked away quickly, afraid to catch the manic gleam in their eyes she'd seen in so many of her neighbors.

A large building, larger even than the council chamber, loomed before them. Light poured from its enormous windows. Artyem took the steps leading up to the huge double doors two at a time. A man stood at the door, dressed in beautiful, well-made slacks, shirt and jacket. She thought he must be someone of importance as he opened the door for them.

The inside of the house was magnificent. Emya could hardly take it all in. Bright white stone lined the floor, and the walls were colored a light blue. They ascended a curved staircase with a banister of ornately carved poles and smooth railing. Detailed paintings of richly-dressed people in dark wood frames lined the walls. If only she could have stopped to admire them, but she was falling behind Artyem's unrelenting pace. Past the stairs, they walked down a hall with wooden floors. She couldn't believe she was stepping on something as precious as wood, but the village was on the edge of a forest, so their attitude must have been a little different. Artyem, now a distance ahead of her, pushed open the door at the end of the hall.

"What happened?" Emya heard a woman say as she caught up.

"He's been attacked by the Faolgal," replied Artyem.

Emya entered the room as Artyem laid Felix in a small, clean bed. A woman in a white dress sat on the edge and examined him. Artyem stepped back.

"There is much more wrong with him than an attack from the Faolgal," the woman said, looking over him with a practiced eye.

"If there wasn't, he would not have been attacked in the first place," Artyem said flatly.

"What was he doing there?"

"That I do not know, but I will find out."

Abruptly he took Emya by her arm, twirled her around, and marched her out. In the hallway, he pushed her back against the wall and towered over her, blocking escape. He was more intimidating in the light. His heavy clothes were scratched and scorched like flesh. A belt encircled his waist, two long knives, and a sword secured in it. Even more unsettling was his face, which had one long scar that ran from his cheek to a mangled ear before disappearing into his short, black hair. Despite this, his features, though grim and scrutinizing, were youthful. He couldn't have been much older than Emya or Felix.

"Who are you and how did you come to be with him?" He jutted his chin in the direction of the room where Felix lay unconscious.

"My village," she said in a quiet voice. "He was there. We escaped together."

"Your village held him captive?" he asked in stark disbelief. Emya shook her head quickly.

"He came with savage men. They made themselves our leaders and brought him with them as their captive. They were using him for..." she couldn't bring herself to tell him. What if Felix didn't want his secret to be revealed? What if Artyem hated magic too? He might kill Felix, and her for good measure. Or he might want to take their magic, as his fearsome appearance reminded her of the Kings.

"For what?" he pressed impatiently. "I need to know what they did to him."

Emya wrapped her arms around herself and stared at the floor. If she did not tell him, he might harm her. If she did tell him, the same result. She could feel him watching her, looming. The world seemed to close in around her, encasing the two of them in a tiny box with no escape. She tottered a little.

"We can't help him unless we know what's been done to him," he said more gently. She looked up through her lashes. He'd taken a step back and was looking at her a little less severely.

The words wouldn't come; too long had she suppressed them. Only once had she let them out and the Kings had taken advantage of her for it. She could not let that happen again.

The door opened behind them and the woman stuck her head out. Artyem half turned.

"I know what is wrong," she said. "You can stop interrogating her."

Artyem relaxed, visibly relieved. "Can you help

71

him?"

"Yes, but he will need weeks to recover."

Artyem sighed in relief. "He can take all the time he needs, but I doubt it will be more than a week or two."

Shaking her head in disbelief, the woman disappeared into the room, closing the door behind her. Artyem turned back to Emya.

"You're going to tell me what happened," he said, his voice soft but firm. "But it can wait for now. Come."

He turned and strode away. With no choice but to follow, she trotted after him. Through a maze of halls and corridors, he led her up another flight of stairs to a nondescript wooden door. Opening it, he gestured for her to enter.

Inside was a comfortably sized room, a large, plush bed, a table against the wall with one chair, and a washbasin. Emya turned, Artyem had not followed her in.

"Get some sleep. We'll talk in the morning." He shut the door, his heavy boots thudding on the floor as he retreated. Like the Kings, he ordered her about with no explanation. With a long sigh, she sank onto the floor, tears welling up. She pushed the heels of her hands against her eyes. Her shoulder and head pulsed with pain and blood soaked her clothing. She couldn't bring herself to lie in the bed and get the beautiful blankets dirty and bloody. For a long while she sat like that until there was a gentle tap on the door. It opened without waiting for her response.

"Oh, my dear," said the woman who'd taken charge of Felix. "You're as much as a mess as poor Felix. Worry not, I'll take care of you."

Emya was silent except for hisses of pain that escaped her lips as the woman cleaned and bandaged her shoulder. Then she helped Emya up and guided her to the washbasin where she washed Emya's hair and wounded scalp. She applied a soothing salve to the gash and wrapped her head in a towel.

"Here's a nightdress," she said, handing her a neatly folded bundle. "You can take a proper bath tomorrow; do you need help getting changed?"

Emya shook her head and the woman wished her good night. She should have asked the woman to help her dress. Hot tears beaded in her eyes from the searing pain in her shoulder as she pulled her shirt over her head. Thankfully the nightdress buttoned up in the front. She slid her injured arm into the sleeve without too much complaint from her shoulder. Feeling a little better, she crawled into bed.

Chapter Six

Never had she slept in a more comfortable bed. Morning light flooded the room, but nothing could coax her out of that cloud of soft blankets. Or so she thought until a scent most heavenly wafted in. She sat up and contemplated the door.

Though she was unsure about wandering through the enormous house on her own, her stomach growled impatiently. She swung her legs off the bed reluctantly and crept over to the door and tried the knob. Unlocked. Cracking the door open, she peered out and found the hallway empty. Encouraged, she slipped out and crept skittishly down the hall.

It was like a maze, twisting and turning, but eventually, she found the stairs she was certain they had ascended last night. As she descended, two tall women in white and blue dresses of a sturdy material appeared, going up. Too late to run back up the stairs, she pressed herself against the wall. As they walked by, they smiled at her but did not stop to ask her what she was doing in the house.

She wondered how much that man, Artyem, had told them about their mysterious guests. Certainly, he hadn't told them to keep her locked up, unwise though it seemed. They couldn't know she wasn't going to try to rob them. This house was a place any thief would dream of being left alone in. Where Artyem was now she did not know. She was more concerned if Felix was alright, but the house had so many rooms that she could not begin to look for him without getting caught. She didn't want to anger the unknown but obviously important occupants of the magnificent house. Though she wanted nothing more than to find Felix and ask him what they should do next, he was in a bad way the night before and it was impossible that he'd recovered enough to leave.

There was no one about as she padded softly through the silent, empty halls. The first rays of morning light bathed the wood-paneled walls in dreamy warm light. She could not imagine one person or family owning such a house. It might have been a council chamber supported by the whole village.

As she descended the last set of stairs, she found the entrance hall deserted. She'd passed through so quickly the night before that she'd hardly seen it, but she was sure it was the main entrance. Two grand double doors were set on a wall that had windows looking out over the village while each of the two adjacent walls had one tall, plain white door. The wall opposite had a set of ornately carved and gilded doors.

Her nose, and the sounds of talking and clanking dishes, led her to the door on her right. A cheerful scene greeted her. In the middle of the large kitchen a long, sturdy wooden table was set with plates of food, roasted meats, potatoes, eggs, bread, and foods she'd never seen before. Her watering mouth and growling stomach urged her to go in, but at least a dozen people sat around the table.

Artyem sat amidst them, looking grim. He did not smile when he saw her. The rest of the group greeted her with wide smiles and wishes of good morning. An elderly man with neatly trimmed hair and beard beckoned to her.

"Good morning young lady, welcome to my home."

"Come sit down and have some breakfast," said an equally aged woman seated next to him. Emya was frozen in the doorway. Never had she been greeted with such enthusiasm and she didn't trust it. How quickly would the smiles change to disgust and anger if they found out she had magic?

"She's frightened," one of the ladies next to Artyem said. "Artyem must have scared her last night." She rapped him lightly on the arm with a dainty, bejeweled hand. Artyem said nothing, still scrutinizing Emya. A hand on her back gently pushed her into the room. It was one of the women she'd seen on the stairs. The elderly man stood up and beckoned her to take his seat. She did so wordlessly, unsure of how they expected her to behave. Kamala would have had a fit if she'd dared to take a seat from an older person, even if they offered it to her, but Emya couldn't say no to the owner of the house. A fresh plate replaced his and the elderly woman next to her began piling food on it. Everyone at the table resumed their conversations but glanced over at her every so often.

The food was all but irresistible. She glanced over at Artyem. Though he had resumed a conversation with the dainty woman next to him, he kept his gaze fixed on her.

"Eat up, sweetie. You look half-starved," said the elderly woman with an affectionate pat on the shoulder.

Emya shrank away instinctively. The woman's brow knitted together in concern but she said nothing.

At first, she ate small, careful bites so as not to seem rude, but after a few minutes, she couldn't help but tuck in heartily. Everything tasted as delicious as it smelled.

"What's this?" Emya asked, softly pointing to a yellow curved food that appeared to be some sort of fruit.

"It's called a banana. They don't grow around here but we have a special greenhouse for them." The old woman peeled off the tough outer skin and handed it to her. She took a small, experimental bite. Sweet, soft, and delicious, she at the whole thing in moments.

"What is your name, sweetie?" the old woman asked, pouring a liquid from a jug on the table and placing it in front of Emya.

"Emya." She took a sip from the cup. It was a sweet juice she had never tasted.

"That's a lovely name. I'm Mrs. Mellia."

Emya stopped eating to gape at her. No one had ever called her name lovely, or anything else about her for that matter. Mrs. Mellia must have mistaken her disbelief for embarrassment because she patted her on the shoulder again and chuckled.

"Excuse the outspokenness of an old woman. I hope you will be comfortable while you stay in my home. I think Artyem would prefer if you do."

"I will speak to her after breakfast," Artyem said, his tone was polite but there was a hint of foreboding in his words.

"If you must," Mrs. Mellia said. Then, noticing the worried look in her eyes, she added quietly to Emya, "Don't worry, my dear. No harm will come to you while you're in my house."

"I'm not going to harm her," Artyem said

indignantly. "Not unless she gives me a very good reason."

"I think you should stop talking if you're going to say things like that," Mrs. Melia said sternly.

Artyem looked as though he was about to tell her that he would say anything he wanted, but he thought better of it. "My apologies," he said.

Emya ate until she was fuller than she ever remembered being her entire life. Indeed, she could hardly stand up as the women in blue and white cleared the dishes away and the rest of the diners rose and drifted from the table. She looked down at her stomach. Though flat as it had always been, it felt like a great melon rested within. Dark boots appeared before her suddenly. She had not heard Artyem get up or approach.

"Come," he said without expression. He led her from the table into a short corridor where he stopped at a heavy wooden door and held it open for her. Inside was a large room with shelves filled with more books than her whole village owned. Opposite the door were clear crystal windows that stretched from floor to ceiling. Large chairs covered in the same material as the guard's clothes were placed around the room, though most of them were near the windows to take advantage of the natural light for reading. A large square table with six chairs drew the eye to the center of the room. It was covered in open books, papers, and things that she did not know the name or function of.

Artyem stepped in and closed the door. He gestured for her to take a seat at the table while he took the one opposite. Folding his hands in front of him, he gave her an assessing look.

"It is my duty to determine whether or not you pose a threat to Felix or anyone else in this village," he said flatly. "You will tell me your story from the moment you discovered Felix to the moment I found you. You will answer my questions. I will determine if you are lying, and believe me," he leaned forward his eyes narrowed, "I will know if you are lying."

Thoroughly intimidated, Emya stared at him wide-eyed and silent.

"Well?" He leaned back in his chair, folding his arms across his chest.

Voice quavering, she told him how the Kings had come to her village. When she got to how she had come to be their student she hesitated. She did not want to tell him about learning magic.

"They noticed me," she said. "They wanted to teach me. During their instruction I discovered Felix. They held him captive and I wasn't supposed to talk to him."

She went on to tell him about the festival.

"What did they teach you?" he interrupted.

Her voice caught in her throat.

"They knew many things, from their travels. They taught me about the world."

"Did they teach you about Cada?"

Emya stared at him, mouth slightly gaping as she tried to unravel his meaning.

"No," she said at last.

"Vannoh? Brahin? Trebsil?" He continued to list strange words she didn't understand.

"No," she said, cowed. He leaned forward again, a slight smirk on his face.

"I can tell when the most practiced spy is lying, but I don't need any skill to be able to tell you are not a good liar."

Heat flushed her cheeks.

"Those are all ancient and famous strongholds. Any travelers of the world would know their names. The Kings, as you call them, were not imparting that knowledge on you, clearly. What were they teaching you?"

Emya looked at her hands folded in her lap. She felt as she had when Azo had interrogated her about the well. The same feeling she had when she'd faced the Kings in the throne room before they made her their pupil. This man was no different from them.

"Magic." The word was barely audible. Her shoulders sagged in defeat. She looked up through her eyelashes. His expression was not angry or triumphant. It was not as she expected it to be at all. He looked more confused than anything.

"You can do magic?" he asked slowly. She nodded. "Why do you want to conceal it?"

She was silent, reluctant to answer, afraid of a trap. But he said she had to answer.

"I'm afraid it will make you angry. You will hurt me."

He cocked his head, eyes narrowed, calculating.

"I have given my word I wouldn't harm you unless you gave me a good reason. Nothing you've said so far is a reason to hurt you, least of all because you can do magic."

She nodded. The Kings gave their word that they wouldn't harm her either, and she'd believed them. When he didn't speak again for a few moments, she looked up. He was watching her, contemplating.

"Continue with your story," he said, more kindly.

It was easier to tell him the truth. She had no idea how she was going to tell him while leaving out all the magic. She expected him to interrupt when she told him about the companion, but he allowed her to finish her story.

"This object," he said. "It is in your possession?"

"Yes, it's in my bag." In a panic, she realized that her bag was still in the room she'd slept in. She realized it may not have been the smartest thing to leave it behind, but he didn't seem bothered.

"I will leave it with you. Since your life is dependent on it, but you must not tell anyone here about it."

"I wasn't going to," she said. "Will they search my bag?"

"No." He sat back and rested his chin on his fist, contemplating the shelves. "I'm sorry," he said at last with the utmost sincerity. "You have been through much pain and hardship. I should not have treated you with such hostility. Your information will help us treat Felix and speed his recovery."

Relief flowed through her, though she wished to see him for herself. She wasn't yet sure if she could trust Artyem. Confused and unsure, she longed to talk to Felix. He would know what to do, and he could tell her who Artyem was if he knew.

"You can stay in this house until he is well enough to travel. Mr. and Mrs. Mellia are happy to have you. You can go into the village as well if you wish, but do not wander out."

"I can't," she said. "If I leave and take the companion with me, Felix will die."

"Even more so then," he said with a grim smile. Emya looked down at her lap again. "Do you have any questions?" He waited patiently while she mulled over everything. She had many questions. Too many. More than she had the strength to ask.

"What are those?" She gestured at the windows.

"Those are windows," he said, his brow furrowing in confusion.

"I mean what are they made of? I've never seen anything as clear as water but solid as stone."

"That's called glass. It's made from heating sand, like metal," he said. "Your village doesn't have glass?"

"No," she said. "Did you know Felix could do magic before I told you?"

"Yes, I did. He's very good at it, too. One of the best mages I've ever met. Though he's still young."

"You've met other mages?"

He nodded. "I've met many. I am a guard of Civim, the Citadel of the Mage. Where many mages live and train."

"They teach them? Like the Kings?"

"They teach them, yes, but they are not like your Kings."

Emya nodded her head. He must have been catching on that her incessant head bobbing was a tell that she didn't really believe him.

"I promise. They don't want to take your magic," he said. "Do you have any more questions?"

She shook her head. She wanted to go back to that bedroom to make sure the companion was safe and then find someone to ask about taking a bath.

Artyem had duties to fulfill and spent most of his days away but checked on Felix every night. Emya was rarely allowed to see him as his caretakers didn't want her to get underfoot. That, at least, was something she understood in this baffling, new world. On the occasions she was permitted to see him, he was awake but was too weak to talk for long. In what little conversation they'd had he encouraged her to explore the village. Despite his reassurance, she did not leave the house for several days, too nervous of the other villagers and what they would do—especially if they found out she had magic. A steady stream of neighbors entering the house every day soon diminished her fears.

At first, she spent a considerable amount of time

in the library. She liked the large windows and it initially seemed a good place to keep out of the way. Soon she discovered that most of the visitors to the house were there to peruse the library. It was also where Mr. Mellia spent an hour every day discussing business with important members of the community, though he didn't mind if she sat in. Emya learned that he was the leader of the village. They called him the Mayor and didn't have councilors like her village.

Some villagers were fascinated by Emya. They asked her about where she came from and invited her to their homes for meals. At first, she found these invitations suspicious. Why would they invite a stranger into their homes? She feared they were trying to lure her into a trap. Though she divulged little information and refused their invitations, they smiled pleasantly and expressed wishes to see her around the village soon. Gradually she decided they were just being friendly.

"They'll be picking flowers for Star Night," Mrs. Mellia said two weeks after Emya arrived. "I'm sure they could use some extra help."

Emya looked up from her eggs and toast with a frown. "Star Night?"

"It's our most important holiday. There will be a party under the stars with food, music, and dancing late into the night. Would you mind helping with the flowers?"

Reluctant to leave the safety of the house she only agreed because she knew it would be rude to refuse a request from her gracious host. So, after breakfast, Emya ventured into the village.

The village was very charming in the daylight—much grander than her original impression. The streets were paved with flat, smooth red bricks and were wider than the dirt paths through Emya's village. Every house had a lush green garden with colorful fruits, vegetables, and flowers. Women in brightly colored dresses tended the gardens, chatting with each other over vine-covered fences. They smiled and waved at Emya as she passed by and seemed entirely unperturbed when she did not smile back.

It seemed impossible that anything sinister could exist in this paradise, but Emya kept her guard up. Looming over the peaceful settlement stretched the dangerous, enchanted forest, its towering redwoods silent sentries to the monsters lurking beyond. None of the villagers seemed particularly bothered by it, but Emya still couldn't shake her feeling of unease—not only with proximity to the forest but with herself. Although the villagers seemed to know Felix, they didn't know her. It was possible they only accepted her because she had arrived with him. They would be wise to be wary of an unknown person from a dangerous magical place.

Likewise, Emya was wary of the overly pleasant villagers. She'd seen the consequences of dangerous, unchecked magic, so she kept an eye out for any odd behavior. But to her, all their behavior seemed odd, as they were not scolding her or sending her away. Not yet. A more happy and carefree people she could not imagine.

Rounding the corner of the last house on the street, Emya stopped and stared, her mouth agape. Three large greenhouses glittered in the sunshine. Panes of glass slightly larger than her hand were set like thin bricks in metal frames. Inside she could see flower beds, bushes, and vines being trimmed away by several dozen villagers. If she didn't know better, she would have thought it was a magical illusion. Competing desires to go inside and to avoid the villagers fought inside her as she approached the entrance. Regardless of how she felt, Mrs. Mellia expected her to help, and she was reluctant to disobey her.

"Hello," a woman in a pale green dress greeted her as she pushed through the door.

"Kama… er, Mrs. Mellia sent me." She blushed at her slip of the tongue. Mrs. Mellia was nothing like Kamala, and it had been a long time since she answered to the cruel councilor. Still, her name slipped out and the idea of mistaking pleasant Mrs. Mellia for that mean old hag filled Emya with shame.

"Wonderful," replied the woman. "Come with me."

Emya was led through a maze of flowers and trees being pruned of their flowers by brightly dressed villagers. Men, women, and children all worked side-by-side, chatting happily as flowers fell from their hands into curved wicker baskets. The woman came to a halt in front of a large bed of flowers that Emya recognized. Atop their dark green stems sat a sunshine yellow flower with pointed petals encircling a cup-shaped corona.

A girl around her age looked up and greeted them.

"Hi," she said cheerfully.

"Mrs. Mellia sent a helper," the woman replied. "This is Emya."

Though she had not told the woman her name, Emya was not surprised she knew it.

"This is my daughter Evris. She will show you what to do."

Evris's mother left them to it, hurrying off to direct some boys in a patch of roses.

"You're the visitor," Evris said with curiosity. Emya nodded. "We don't get many travelers here except from the mountains, and we know them all pretty well now."

Evris showed Emya how to cut at the base of the plant so the flower had a nice long stem, and to lay it carefully into the basket with the flowers all facing one way.

"These are the most important flowers for the party," she explained. "We have to be very gentle with them. They're called star flowers, and it is Star Night after all."

"In my village, they're called 'daffodils,'" Emya said quietly. Evris looked surprised but she hid it quickly. No doubt she thought Emya couldn't speak as some of the others had assumed.

"Yes, I've heard them called that too. Both are lovely names, I think."

They picked flowers for some time. Evris hummed while she worked and did not pester Emya, though sometimes Emya caught her looking at her as though she longed to ask questions. After a while, Emya started to relax as the sweet fragrance of flowers, warm air, and quiet, the simple task put her at ease.

"What is the Star Night?" she asked finally.

"It's our most important holiday. The flowers represent everyone living today. We use them to decorate and to honor the stars, which represent the souls of everyone who has ever lived and died."

"In my village, they say when someone dies a star disappears from the sky," Emya said. "I don't know if it's true though."

"Lots of cultures have similar beliefs about the stars. Some believe that when a person dies, they become a star. We don't believe that. The stars are just a symbol."

"It's a nice idea though," Emya said.

With the floodgate of conversation open, Evris asked her about where she had come from. Emya told her, sticking to neutral details and leaving out any mention of magic or mistreatment from the villagers.

"We don't have a lot of wood because we have to go so far to get it or wait for traders to bring it," Emya said. "I've never seen houses made of wood."

"We take wood from the mountains over yonder." Evris pointed out of the greenhouse where a mountain range cut through the land much further away than the enchanted forest.

"Some of the older houses were built before our ancestors came here, like Mrs. Mellia's. Those homes were built using wood from the Sanguine Forest before it was saturated in dark magic. No one can take wood from there anymore. It's cursed."

"That's where we came from," Emya said without thinking. She regretted it the moment she saw the shocked look on Evris's face.

"Wow," she said. She almost seemed impressed, which surprised Emya. Evidently, it was not yet known to everyone that she had come from the forest. "What was it like?"

"Big red trees, mossy grass, and a few shrubs were the only plants. There was no long grass or weeds. It felt unnatural."

Evris crooned in delighted fear.

"I've heard stories about fearsome creatures."

"Yes, we were attacked by something called a Faolgal."

Evris gasped.

"How frightening! But you were with Felix. I'm sure he defeated the foul creature with the last of his strength."

"No," she said, "He was too weak. Artyem saved us."

"Oh well," her smile turned mischievous. "He's a strong warrior, and very handsome too, don't you think?"

Taken aback, Emya hummed a halfhearted agreement, if only not to hurt Evris's feelings. She hadn't noticed if Artyem was handsome or not. She'd hardly looked at his face, she'd been too scared of him to even consider that, and Felix looked half-dead. She did not think that was a very handsome look.

They cleared the whole daffodil bed by lunchtime and delivered their baskets to the cart outside the greenhouses. There were heaps of flowers, all headed to a large field outside the village, where set up was well underway for the party.

"You're coming tonight, aren't you?" Evris asked.

Emya was surprised to find she didn't want to disappoint Evris, but she also felt she would rather avoid a large group of reveling villagers. Images of villagers, dancing, and fighting drunk with enchantment superimposed on the charming little village in her mind.

"I might," she murmured, expecting Evris to protest earnestly and beg for her commitment. Instead, Evris just smiled.

"Then I might see you there."

She bid her goodbye at the steps of Mrs. Mellia's house.

Chapter Seven

In the entrance hall, one of the white-clad healers—as she'd discovered they were called—was passing through to the kitchen before coming to a stop when she caught sight of Emya.

"Felix is asking for you," she said. "I told him I'd send you in when you got back. Have some lunch then you can see him."

Emya tried to object. She wanted to see him right away, but the healer insisted. After inhaling the delicious food, Emya hurried up the stairs to Felix's room.

He was sitting up at least, though his face was still pale and gaunt. His hands were folded in his lap and trembling. Artyem sat in a chair next to the bed. He stood abruptly when he saw Emya and went to stand in the corner. He leaned against the wall, arms crossed, while Emya took his seat.

"We were just talking about you," Felix said in a voice so strong and clear that she barely recognized it.

"What about me?" she asked lightly. Seeing him alive and recovering lifted a weight from her heart. If he had died, she didn't know what she would have done.

"We were discussing whether or not you would still like to accompany us to Civim to learn magic. After your experience with Azo and Fen, Artyem thought you might rather settle here."

Emya glanced at Artyem. He was very astute considering they'd talked so little.

"I like it here," she said, surprising herself, "but I have to learn magic, don't I? Or I'll die."

Felix gave a little chuckle.

"You shouldn't believe everything they told you," he said with a sad smile. "If you don't use your magic it will eventually dry up, but it won't kill you."

She wasn't surprised that the Kings had lied to her. Still, she hesitated. There was no proof that Felix wasn't lying to her either. She trusted him because she had to, but that didn't mean she believed everything he said—especially when she could not make sense of it. She didn't want to risk death if she chose not to use her magic.

"What about the companion?" she asked. "We can't be separated."

Felix grimaced, exchanging a look with Artyem.

"Yes. We must find a solution to that, but in the meantime, you can set up a new life. I believe I can extend the distance we can be separated from the object. I think I could stretch it far enough so that you could stay here."

"In which case you must stay here longer than you wish," Artyem said in a low voice. Evidently, this was an unresolved discussion. "You cannot perform magic like that until you are entirely recovered."

"So be it if Emya wants to stay here," he said, though it sounded like a concession for her sake. The matter was not settled.

Though the beautiful little village and its kind people had grown on Emya, she knew she could not settle there with the shadow of the companion looming over her. She feared that shadow would spread and shroud the village. There was only one clear path: to follow Felix until they freed themselves of the object or it killed them.

Besides, she *did* want to learn magic. Despite believing her entire life had been cursed by possessing magic, she had never felt better than when she was doing it. That was part of the reason she had trusted the Kings so entirely and had been willing to turn a blind eye to Felix's suffering and warnings. Though if learning magic twisted her conscience to the point where she did not care that someone was suffering such cruelty then perhaps that was a reason she should not learn magic.

"I will go with you." She took out the object which she carried in her pocket every day. "I want to see this through. I can't stand the idea of waiting around in hopes that one day I'll be free of it."

Felix smiled approvingly. Artyem looked even more grim than usual but made no comment. Nothing could ever make him happy, she decided.

"Then you shall come with us to the Citadel Civim," said Felix.

"There is one other thing you wished to ask her, Felix," Artyem said. Felix looked confused for a moment.

"Oh yes. Will you go to the Star Night party?"

"Well, I... I don't think I want to," she said.

"I didn't think you would, but I think you should go. I promise it will be different from the festival at your village," Felix replied.

"Alright," she said, unwilling to argue.

91

As twilight set in, Emya donned the cloak Mrs. Mellia lent her for the chilly night, then checked her pocket for the ever-present companion, and made her way downstairs. Waiting in the entrance hall, to her surprise, was Evris. She looked elegant, wearing a pink dress embroidered with tiny roses and flowers braided in her chestnut hair, and greeted Emya excitedly.

"I came to see if you were coming. Mrs. Mellia said you were. She seemed glad I'd come along. She didn't want you to go alone. Want to come with me?"

"Oh. Yes," Emya said, relieved. She had planned to follow someone to the party, for she did not know where it was exactly, except that it was outside the village, toward the mountains.

"Let's get going then if you're ready," said Evris. "The party will have already started by the time we get there."

"Is it bad to be late?" Emya asked with worry.

"No. It just means less time for dancing," Evris said excitedly.

Outside, the streets were no longer bathed in the light. Instead, impenetrable darkness filled the village and a sense of dread filled Emya.

"Why is it so dark?" she whispered frantically to Evris.

"All the lights in the village are to be put out for the party," she said patiently, taking Emya's hand and pulling her along. "The better to see the stars."

Emya tentatively accepted this explanation, though she wondered why they couldn't take a little candle with them like the ones she saw some of the other villagers carrying. It turned out that Evris didn't need much light to navigate. She led Emya safely past dips and inclines without tripping or stumbling until they emerged from the village. A patch of the vast plane glowed in the distance, a beacon in the dark. Lively music drifted on the gentle breeze.

As they approached, the most heavenly scent of thousands of freshly cut flowers saturated the air. Emya gaped in awe as they passed under an arch of rose vines into the meadow. Garlands of honeysuckle, wisteria, and jasmine cascaded over high fences, secluding the party from the valley. Villagers lounged around low tables covered in crisp white cloths, strewn with flowers and plates of mouthwatering food. A large vase filled with daffodils was placed at the center of each table. Encircled by the tables was a patch of grass quickly being trampled by many exuberant dancing feet, their rhythms encouraged by woodwind and string.

Excitement filled Emya for the first time in longer than she could remember. A smile pulled at her lips, and when she turned to Evris she saw her grinning back at her. They found Evris's mother at a table and helped themselves to the food. It was even more exotic and delicious than what Mrs. Mellia served, though she supposed that it should be for such an important celebration.

Evris tried to take her out to dance but Emya declined. Instead, she stood at the edge of the dancing, watching Evris twirl and stomp with her friends. The brightly colored dresses flowed around the ladies, brushing their partners as they spun. The men wore crisp white shirts, colorful waistcoats and matching trousers, and expertly matched their partners in step and rhythm.

Several young men approached Emya, asking her to dance. She declined as politely as she could, but every offer reminded her of being forced by her friend Adrik into his bewitched waltz.

A few other villagers stood around the dancers, clapping along. Most were older folk who looked as though their bones might rattle apart if they attempted to join the dances, but age had not dampened their enthusiasm. Among the onlookers, Emya spotted Artyem. He was partially obscured by two ladies smiling and batting their lashes at him. He responded to their simpering with polite interest, but when he caught Emya's eye his expression hardened. Excusing himself from the ladies, he weaved through the onlookers and tables until she lost sight of him.

Her heart thumped rapidly. She tried to recall everything she did after speaking to Felix, discovering nothing that could have invoked his ire. Maybe he had hoped she wouldn't have listened to Felix. Maybe he didn't want her at the party. If Felix told him what happened in her village, he might have concluded that she was the cause and would not want her near an innocent gathering of these pleasant folks. Well, she wasn't the cause and she knew it. And if he was going to treat her poorly, she wasn't going to put up with it.

Evris broke away from a boy who'd asked her to dance three times already to join Emya.

"It's so much fun but so tiring," she said, red-faced and panting a little.

"It does look tiring," Emya replied before adding so as not to sound too doleful, "and it does look fun, though I still don't care to try it."

Evris laughed, grasping Emya's arm affectionately. She leaned in and whispered in her ear.

"Did you see Artyem is here? I never thought he would come. He was talking to my cousin and her friends; they're absolutely infatuated with him."

"Why do you think he's come then?" She did not ask if Evris thought he was infatuated in return, for he did not seem like the kind of person who became infatuated with anyone.

"Who can fathom the intent of a guard of the Tritian? Perhaps he is here on orders. Tonight is a special night, after all."

Felix's orders most likely. At that moment a young man approached them and with a charming smile. In no time at all, he swept Evris into the dance once more.

Emya decided to go back to the table. There was still plenty of food and drink, but she had eaten her fill and was beginning to weary. The fragrant air and low light lulled her into a sleepy stupor.

"Do you not wish to dance?" said a soft, low voice. Emya turned to find Artyem had taken a seat next to her.

"No," she said. "Do you?"

"No."

They sat in silence for a few moments, watching the dancers.

"You don't want me to learn magic, do you?" Emya asked. "That's why you suggested to Felix that I stay here."

"I suggested you stay here because I thought you would want to," he said, dodging the question.

"Should I continue learning magic?"

He looked thoughtful for a moment.

"I cannot tell you. As many who choose to study magic, an equal number choose to forsake it. Many believe that magic is destroying our world. I'm inclined to agree."

This came as a shock to Emya. Artyem was loyal to Felix and knew more about magic than she did. Ignorance was the primary reason her village feared magic, or so she believed. Maybe they knew more about it than she thought.

"How can that be?" she asked.

"There is magic in the world that is wild. It

cannot be controlled or contained. This kind of magic is dismantling civilizations and driving men mad." He gestured towards the enchanted forest. "It's infected that forest. From what you've told me, it's poisoned your village. It might be better for all of us if no one practiced magic any longer." He sighed. "But that is not up to me. If you wish to learn magic, then you shall."

The music, almost constant since her arrival, trilled to an end and all went quiet. The lights were extinguished one by one.

"Come," he said. "It's time."

Everyone gathered in the center of the meadow, now a patch of churned up grass and dirt. Emya found Evris who took her by the arm and led her to the center of the group where all the ladies were gathered. Artyem stood just behind Emya with the gentlemen. As the last light was extinguished everyone looked up at the sky, illuminated by twinkling stars cascading from horizon to horizon.

A low baritone humming arose from the outer circle, joined by soft, low chanting. Then a high soprano in the center sang a hauntingly beautiful melody. Emya didn't understand the words, but they sounded sad yet content. Evris was singing too, her voice in Emya's ear was clear and sweet.

The song lasted several minutes and then ended with the voices dropping out until the baritone humming drifted into silence. Everyone stood in silence. Emya gazed at the sky, trying to make out constellations. A gentle tap on the shoulder interrupted her musings. She turned and found that Artyem had moved closer. He pointed up toward the north where, she hadn't noticed, the party had turned to watch.

Only the outline of the mountain range was visible in the dark. Looming and silent, every gaze was fixed on it. Then, as if bidden by some unseen signal, lights burst into the air above the highest peak. Thousands of lights flickered in and out of existence, spreading from peak to peak in patterns.

"The lights tell a story," Artyem said in a low voice. "About how the mage came to be, their journey into this land, and their relationship with the people of this village, who came before them."

"How long have the mage been here?" Emya whispered over her shoulder.

"Over a millennium."

"That long?"

And the village had existed even longer. It was impossible to imagine a small, quiet settlement existing for a thousand years. Only fortresses and great cities achieved such a status. Her own village had been established only some generations before, and no doubt would be abandoned before the end of the next. Settlements didn't last long as the barely tenable land would no longer bear crops in less than a hundred years.

"Mages were neither born nor bred," Artyem said, pointing to the lights as they burst into existence and flickered out. Try as she might, she couldn't see how the illuminations told the story. "They found magic trapped in the world in the form of nature and elements. They studied the phenomenon it took the form of—a ripple in a river that healed the sick, a vein of gold in a mountain that never ran dry, a flower that never dies—until they determined how to extract it.

"Once loose, magic searched for a new dwelling, which it found inside the ones who released it. With magic, they changed the world to their desire, creating kingdoms, building armies, fighting wars, dividing and uniting at their whim."

The white lights turned to red, orange, and gold.

"All the people of the world became subjugated to the most powerful of the mage. Kingdoms fought and destroyed each other at the whim of their mage lords. Locked away in their strongholds, the mages studied and experimented with magic. They concentrated it into objects, creating powerful and unfathomable tools of war.

"I do not think even they completely understood how their creations worked," he added as the lights went out only to return in sickly green and purple.

"When all the kingdoms of the world and their armies were spent, the mages fought each other. Terrible battles scarred the land with permanent curses. Mages employed their strongest and most devastating magical weapons to best one another until the power became uncontrollable and consumed them. With the end of the mage, the use of magic was lost. It existed only in a raw form. Separated from its original, natural state, it had become uncontrollable."

All lights extinguished except for a pinpoint of yellow light shooting out from the highest peak. The weight of the object nestled in Emya's pocket became uncomfortably heavy.

"Magic, it seemed, had destroyed all that was good. Yet out of the ruin of the world emerged a remnant of humanity. With no desire for riches, power, or magic, they searched for a place where they could live in simplicity and peace."

Twinkling sparks of light played across the mountain.

"Some went out into the world and found others like them building new lives, and then..."

Sparks of blue light mingled with the white.

"Magic was found again in nature in the form of a newborn baby. His parents were frightened. If anyone found out, their child would be killed. They raised him in secret, teaching him to be good, kind, and honest. They impressed upon him the desire to help those weaker than himself. But he did not want to hide all his life. As a man, he left home to find others like him, and find them he did. Some were kept secret, like him, some were feared and mistreated, as his parents had feared he would be, and some came from happy families. Together they honed their skills and sought out other mages. They found a place where they could live in peace and safety, for they had many enemies, and built a citadel for their kind. Civim."

He pointed to the tallest mountain in the range.

"And there they reside, a place for mage and magic." A burst of blue light shined over the tallest peak. "A guardian of rebirth." A single ray of light shot across the sky in an arc over the village.

The field fell into silent darkness. A low murmur erupted as the villagers began to leave the meadow.

"I never knew that," said Evris. "I knew the basic story, but I never knew all those other things."

"That's because we rarely have a translator for the mage's language of light." Emya hadn't noticed Mr. Mellia standing beside Artyem.

"It's very interesting, don't you think?" Evris nudged Emya in the ribs.

Emya could not answer. A large lump occluded her throat.

"We'd better head back," Mr. Mellia said jovially. "Don't want to be wandering around alone out here at night. Although with a Tritium Guard in our company I'm sure we're perfectly safe."

"Don't make such assumptions," said Artyem as they joined the throng making their way up the valley towards the village. "I'm only one person and you are three to defend."

"I think it's terrible how some of the new mages were treated," Evris opined. "It wasn't their fault they had magic."

"I agree," Artyem said. "Though you can't imagine how the entire world suffered. Right and wrong were skewed and twisted in the minds of the survivors. Many no longer cared to know the difference."

"Not here though," Evris said. "We've always lived in peace with the mages of Civim."

"Not always," Mr. Mellia said. "Many generations passed before our ancestors trusted the mages of the citadel and many more before we considered them friends."

"But we've never mistreated anyone born with magic here," Evris said. "Some of the finest mages in Civim have come from here."

"Which is why we eventually became allies," Artyem said.

"We never feared mages born to our community, though in those days there was plenty of reason to. Now, it's quite unthinkable," Mr. Mellia said. Artyem grimaced and glanced sideways at Emya but said nothing. Emya looked at her feet.

"When children started being born with magic, the mages came down from the mountain to convince their mothers to give them away for training. Most agreed, though our records suggest it was mainly out of fear. In hindsight, it's a good thing we did. There still are many dangerous magic wielders in the world—and that forest over there attracts them." Mr. Mellia clapped Artyem on the shoulder proudly. "Good thing we have strong friends to protect us."

"Indeed," Artyem said before changing the subject.

Emya struggled to keep the tears at bay. Her entire life she struggled to understand why her village hated her so, now she finally had the missing piece. Her secluded community was stuck on an old prejudice. Yet with some validity to it, as evidenced by the Kings, and the sanguine forest, and likely many more things she would discover if she continued on this path. That didn't make what they'd done right, but understanding the past a bit more improved her confidence that going to Civim and learning magic was a good decision.

Even so, hot tears trickled down her cheeks, and she was glad for the dark to hide them from Artyem and Evris as she ruminated on the story of the boy with magic. Unlike her parents, who somehow let the whole village know she had magic, his had tried to protect him. He was lucky in a way. She couldn't imagine there were many children born with magic who'd been among the happy back then. Emya pushed her emotions back, yawning, and rubbing the tears away under the guise of fatigue.

By the time she said good night to Evris on the steps of the house, her face felt cool enough not to alarm Evris. She seemed not to notice anything was amiss at all as she hugged Emya and thanked her for coming. Relieved, Emya followed the two men inside.

Mr. Mellia set off down the hall after a cheery good night, and Emya and Artyem climbed the stairs alone.

"I'm sorry if I did anything to upset you," he said. At her indignant look, he quickly went on, "I know you were crying. I can see well in the dark."

"It wasn't you," she said looking at her feet. "It was just the story."

"I thought it might be," he said. "After all, you can relate to it better than anyone here."

He escorted her to her room and bid her good night.

Chapter Eight

Though Felix had grown in strength enough to walk around the house and join them at meals dressed in his bedclothes, he had not yet recovered enough to make the journey up the mountain to the Citadel after a few weeks had passed. Meanwhile, Emya occupied most of her time with Evris, who came by every day to whisk her away. Sometimes the two of them would help in the gardens, while at others they would lounge on a picnic blanket among the wildflowers, gazing up at the mountains and chatting about nothing. Evris was easy to be friends with. She was kind, considerate, and easy to talk to. She even made Emya laugh, and the first time she did, Evris invited her over for dinner.

Evris lived in a smaller house than Mrs. Mellia and many of the other villagers, but it was warm and cheerful. Her mother toiled in the garden and her father did carpentry when he wasn't managing the village cattle. Emya spent at least some of every day at Evris's house.

In the evening, Evris' parents cooked dinner together, singing duets and dancing around the kitchen while their two younger children, Evris's brother and sister, laughed and clapped along. The first time Emya came for dinner she'd thought it was some kind of show for her benefit, but the continued revelry on several dinner invitations after indicated that it was their natural joy.

A month had passed since the night of the Star Night, and Emya received an invitation to a very special dinner with Evris's family, though the reason for the meal was kept a secret. As she prepared in her room Emya examined her reflection in the mirror. It showed every detail perfectly. Emya didn't feel the need to use the mirror very often, as she'd never cared much about her appearance, but when she was going over to Evris's for dinner, Mrs. Mellia had explained that it was customary to look neat and tidy. So Emya brushed through her long black hair—it had grown out considerably since Kamala wasn't around to hack it off—and wiped the dirt off her suntanned face. Satisfied with her appearance, she put on one of the green linen dresses Mrs. Mellia had lent her.

Activity buzzed throughout the Mellia house. As Emya made her way to the front door, she dodged maids carrying laundry, sweeping the floors, and other tidying tasks in preparation for a special event that would take place the following evening. Stepping aside to let past one grimacing maid carrying a heavy statue, Emya turned and bumped into Artyem. He grabbed her by the arm as she stumbled back.

"Sorry," she said.

"It's alright. There are too many people in here." He let go and moved past her.

"Why do they all need to be here? What's so

important about tomorrow?"

A ghost of a smile played across his prematurely hardened features.

"They're having a party," he replied.

"Celebrating what?"

"You," he said with a hint of amusement.

"Me?" she said disconcertingly. She did not think he would tease her so, but maybe he was finally starting to show a sense of humor.

"We're leaving two days from now," he said. "They want to send us off with good food and a little fun." He frowned at her bemused look. "Did no one tell you?"

"No," she breathed.

"Well, that's the plan. Felix can make the journey, though I tried to insist that he take a few more days to rest. Alas, it's not in my power to force him to stay when the healers say he is strong enough to travel."

"Oh. When did they say that?"

Artyem frowned. "Yesterday. He went straight to Mr. Mellia and told him we were leaving."

"I'll have to say goodbye to some people before we go."

"You'll get the chance tomorrow," Artyem said, looking relieved. "Are you going to dinner?"

"Yes."

"I'll let you go then. You don't want to be late."

Emya hadn't been around most of the day before, so it was no wonder they'd forgotten to tell her. Now she sighed as she stepped down the stairs. Her evening would be bittersweet knowing that she'd have to say goodbye to her first close friend, though at least they wouldn't be too far apart.

Evris was waiting for her in the foyer. She was enthusiastically talking, much to Emya's surprise, with Felix. She almost didn't recognize him. He stood tall now, practically towering over Evris. His light brown hair had been washed and brushed and it framed his healthy features. He wore a white shirt and red waistcoat, as was the style, that brought out the color in his cheeks.

"Emya!" Evris ran over and took her by the hand. She dragged her over to Felix. "Felix is coming to dinner with us. My parents invited him."

Though everyone in town seemed to know of Felix, none had seemed to know him well enough to invite him to dinner. They spoke of him as though he was terribly important, which for all Emya knew, he was.

"Yes," he said. "It's well overdue."

He held out his arm and Evris, while still holding Emya's hand, took it.

"You didn't tell me you were coming this morning," Emya said to him.

"I'm sorry. I wasn't sure I'd be able to go. Artyem's overly cautious as ever." He shrugged. That explained Artyem's attitude towards leaving, though Felix looked like an entirely different person now that he was rested. He'd undergone quite the transformation from when he was almost too weak to walk.

"Is Artyem your personal guard?" Evris asked. "I've heard that some of the Tritium act as personal guards to the most important mages."

Felix chuckled. "That they do, but I am not one of those mages."

"Ah well, you don't need one, do you?" Evris asked.

"I never did before, though in light of recent events they may yet assign me one."

"And wouldn't it be funny if it was Artyem?"

"Perhaps, though I don't see that he's done anything to deserve what he would surely see as a punishment," he said with a wink.

"I thought you were friends," Evris said with mock

surprise.

"I think he's my friend, but I cannot say for sure if he thinks the same of me."

"They are friends," Emya chimed in. The pair turned to her. "Artyem tells Felix what to do and Felix ignores him, but they still talk all day long. Artyem fusses over Felix like a mother hen, so they must be friends."

Felix gave a surprised laugh.

"Yes," he said. "That is the only explanation I will accept. It is finally good to know that he considers me a friend."

"Are you making fun of me?" Emya asked.

"No. You've succinctly surmised the nature of our relationship. Artyem is not an easy man to define, but you seem to have uncovered something of his nature better than I have over the years."

It was strange to hear Felix speaking so clearly and confidently, but she was relieved. When they arrived at Evris's house the smell of food wafted out onto the porch to greet them, as did Dini and Breck, Evris's sister and brother. They hugged Emya and Breck held out his hand for Felix to shake. Dini, the youngest, looked shyly up at him from behind Emya's skirt. She giggled uncontrollably when he smiled and wiggled his fingers at her.

"Welcome to our home," Evris mother said, embracing him warmly. Her father, with a little more formality, gave him a firm handshake.

"We're glad to have you," he said.

"Thank you, Mr. Kabris," replied Felix.

They all sat in the parlor while Mrs. Kabris cooked. Instead of joining her in their nightly duet as usual, Mr. Kabris offered Felix a comfortable chair and sat across from him. Emya sat next to Evris on their small, plush couch. She would miss their comfortable furniture that was so unlike the harsh wood and stone furnishings of her village.

"So, you're here to take my precious, oldest daughter away?" Mr. Kabris said sternly, though there was a hint of amusement in his tone. Emya stiffened. Evris hadn't said anything about going away. Perhaps they weren't as good of friends as she'd hoped.

Evris gave her a sideways glance and said jovially, "Father, what have you done? You've gone and given away the surprise!"

"I thought you told Emya," he said, abashed.

"Well the cat's out of the bag," Felix said. "Evris is coming with us to Civim."

"Why?" Emya asked, directing the question at Evris. She grinned broadly for a few moments with unmanageable excitement.

"Can you not guess?" Before Emya could guess anything, she burst out, "to learn magic of course!"

Emya gaped at her.

"You...can do magic?"

"Yes!" She began to talk so fast Emya could hardly keep up. "I discovered it at the beginning of this summer. Father sent word up the mountain and the mages were to send a guard to bring me to Civim as soon as one could be spared. That's the real reason Artyem is here. He was supposed to take me right away, but he was diverted when he got a message that there was someone in danger in the forest and that it might be Felix, who has been missing, but you know about that. Sure enough, he found both of you and it was decided that we would delay my departure until Felix was well enough to make the journey. Oh, I wanted to tell you so bad..." Ervis took both of Emya's hands and looked deep and pleading into her eyes as if begging forgiveness. "But Artyem said I was not to say a word to you until it was certain that he would be able to take all of us. And he said you might not want to come, so I had to wait until everything was settled. Finally, finally, I can tell you!"

Ervis took a deep breath and grinned even wider.

"Well," said Mr. Kabris. "I suppose my scare tactics aren't worth much. I doubt I could stop Evris from going if I wanted to, magic or no."

Felix smiled slyly. "No, I don't think so."

Emya sat in silence while Evris and her father probed Felix with questions about Civim and learning magic. It could not have been random chance that Emya had been introduced to Evris. Emya never told anyone, that she could do magic, yet it could not have been a coincidence that Mrs. Mellia had sent her to Evris's mother in the greenhouse all those weeks ago. Perhaps Artyem had suggested letting her and Evris get to know each other since they might be traveling up the mountain together. Emya did not want anyone to know she had magic. Artyem had agreed not to speak of it and Felix seemed to think it was best kept quiet. Though the villagers had no fear of the mages from Civim, the enchanted forest—and the dangerous mage it attracted—made them wary of foreign mages. Emya didn't think it would bother Evris or her family if they knew she had magic, but fear twisted inside her at the thought of any of them finding out.

Mrs. Kabris called them all into dinner after a while. The food was scrumptious, and Mrs. Kabris had a chance to question Felix as well, though her questions were more personal.

"When did you know you were a mage?" she asked.

"My parents knew the day I was born," he said. "I gave them quite a fright. I levitated right out of my mother's arms."

Everyone laughed.

"Is that normally when you know if a child has

magic?" Mrs. Kabris asked.

"No ma'am. Most don't know until they're about ten. Though it is not unheard of for magic to lay dormant until sixteen, like Evris."

"Oh no," Evris said, her face falling. "Will I be very far behind?"

"At first, but the advantage of age is the ability to understand complicated concepts more easily. You'll pass them all up in no time I'm sure."

"And did you have to come far to learn at Civim?" asked Mr. Kabris.

"No. I was born on the mountain," Felix explained. "My parents are Tritium. I grew up training in Civim as soon as I could walk, even before I could talk."

"So that's why you're so advanced at your age," Mr. Kabris said. "I've never met someone as young as you with your status."

Felix shook his head. "No, I am the first to achieve it."

"And are you going to study magic as well?" Mrs. Kabris asked, turning to Emya.

Fork frozen in midair, her mouth already agape, Emya hesitated. She did not want to lie to Evris's mother, but she could not bring herself to answer.

"Emya is coming as a favor to me to deal with a matter that concerns both of us," Felix said quickly, his tone was no longer friendly but commanding. Emya nodded.

"Well I'm glad you'll be together," Mrs. Kabris said with no trace of awkwardness at the exchange. "You two have become such close friends."

Dinner passed pleasantly and the rest of the evening they sat in the parlor. Mrs. Kabris served a light, sweet pastry, and elderflower tea. Emya sipped the delicately floral tea, savoring it, paying little attention to the conversation. She'd grown to love Mrs. Kabris's tea and cooking. Her heart was heavy at the thought of leaving. Never had she found more comfort than in the little village. If what Felix said was true, she could pass her days quietly here, never using her magic again. Eventually, it would fade away while she built a life she'd never imagined was possible. While the fantasy was a pleasant one, Emya knew better. As long as she was connected to the companion and Felix, her path was tied to them. With the comfort that comes with the knowledge that one's path is set and no other decision could be made, Emya enjoyed the rest of the evening.

The crescent moon was high in the sky as Emya and Felix said good night. Evris offered to walk them home so she could chat Emya's ear off about learning magic. They'd talked about it at length already but Emya didn't mind. Felix walked a little behind them, occasionally chiming in. Now that it was the three of them, Emya felt increasingly guilty for not telling Evris about her magic. She would have to admit it at some point. The longer she waited the more she felt like a bad friend.

The foyer at the Mellia home was bright, clean, and deserted when they arrived. All the maids had either gone home or to bed. Felix bid Evris good night and headed up to his room. Emya watched him ascend the stairs slowly, looking for signs of fatigue. Nothing particularly alarmed her. Alone now, she turned to her friend.

"I have to tell you something," she said quietly.

"Is it a secret?" Evris asked, gleaning from her tone that it was a serious matter.

"Yes, but you're going to find out eventually so I might as well tell you."

"I swear not to tell."

Emya took a deep breath and forced the words out like air from a billow.

"I'm going to learn magic too. At Civim."

Emya wrapped her arms around herself and looked at her feet. It shouldn't have been hard to tell her that. Evris had magic too. But having kept it to herself so long, on top of not answering when her mother asked, made her feel like a liar.

"Oh," Evris said. To Emya's dismay, she sounded a little hurt.

"I'm sorry I didn't tell you at dinner," she mumbled.

"Is that the matter that Felix spoke of?"

Emya looked up in surprise. Evris was watching her, concerned.

"No. That's something else, and I really can't tell you about it. Only that I wish I wasn't involved."

Her look of concern deepened, and dread began to fill Emya. Fear that she'd ruined their friendship chilled her like ice. She'd lied about her powers and made it seem like she was on some sort of special mission that made her more important than Evris, who already felt insecure about being so old when she discovered her magic. Evris put a gentle hand on her arm.

"Why didn't you want to tell us about having magic?" she asked Emya.

"I was afraid."

"Why? My parents wouldn't have been upset, and I certainly wouldn't have. I'm glad to hear that you do. We will be able to learn together."

The dread lifted a little at these words said so sincerely. Evris wasn't hiding any jealousy, but still, there was concern.

"I thought they might be afraid of me," Emya admitted. "Because I have magic and I came from the forest. I thought they might try to hurt me."

Evris knit her brows together in confusion before giving way to understanding and sadness.

"That's what happened in your village." Evris

111

understood now. "They mistreated you out of fear, just like the story."

Emya nodded with a lump in her throat. Evris threw her arms around her in a fierce embrace. Emya hugged her back, forcing the unshed tears away.

"I won't tell anyone," she said, breaking away and holding Emya at arm's length. "No one here will hurt you for having magic. We've lived in the shadow of the Trivim mountain and the Red Forest. We're used to magic, and everyone in the village knows you're not a danger. But I won't tell. You don't have to worry."

Feeling both silly and relieved, Emya thanked Evris. They embraced again, this time in good night, and Evris disappeared into the dark, homebound. Emya fell into bed, not happy or content, but at least feeling a little more confident.

~~*~*~*~*

"My best seamstress helped me make it." Mrs. Mellia laid the bright blue dress out on the bed, arranging it so all the best features were visible. Embroidered patterns in silver thread swirled along the skirt and cuffs; the cloth shimmered like water.

"For me to wear tonight?" Emya asked, never had she imagined wearing anything so beautiful.

"Of course! It is a special occasion."

Mrs. Mellia insisted she try it on. The fluid material slid over her like a gentle stream. Twirling the skirt in front of the mirror, she admired how well it fit. She hardly recognized herself.

"It's so beautiful," she said, turning to Mrs. Mellia. "Thank you."

The old lady looked much younger when she

blushed and chuckled.

"You're welcome, my dear. And after the party, I'll pack it for you so it doesn't get wrinkled or ruined. This material is very durable and requires little care if you store it correctly. Just hang it up when you arrive and it will never need to be washed or ironed unless you spill something on it, then all you have to do is run it under cold water for a few minutes."

Emya tried to listen to the instructions and commit them to memory, but it was difficult as she was burning with astonishment.

"I get to keep it?" she stammered when Mrs. Mellia finished.

"Of course. You get to keep all the clothes we made you. Who else is going to wear them?"

Emya had assumed everything she'd be given was borrowed, much as everything Kamala gave her had been, though she couldn't imagine Mrs. Mellia striking her the way Kamala had if she tried to take anything.

"More importantly, how could I let a young woman leave my house with nothing but the clothes on her back?"

"That's... not all I have," she said, glancing at the drawer where her bag containing her matches, a knife, and the companion had been tucked safely away.

"And not much else," she added. "They're gifts. I hope you will accept them."

Emya nodded then added sincerely, "I've never received such wonderful gifts. Thank you very much."

As twilight fell, Emya met Felix and Artyem at the top of the stairs. Both were dressed stylishly. Felix looked as comfortable as ever in their attire, but Artyem looked out of place in the clothes and his expression suggested he felt so. She preferred him in his regular dark, rugged clothing. Felix looked tired. She hadn't thought dinner the previous night had been very strenuous for him, but he'd stayed in bed well into the morning and then sat in the library most of the day, hardly moving. Maybe she was just worrying too much. Felix broke into a broad grin when he saw her. Artyem smiled politely.

"You look great," Felix said. "I heard they made you a formal dress, very pretty."

"Thanks," Emya said. "It's the most beautiful thing I've ever worn. Although that's not saying much."

Felix offered her his arm and they descended the stairs, Artyem following. Felix led her across the foyer to the tall double doors that she had never been through.

Felix pushed the doors inward revealing a stunning room. Painted white with blue trim, it stretched twice the length and width of her village's council hall. Silver and gold and glass twisted and twirled in beautiful patterns above them. Bright candles burned. Illuminated beneath were three-tiered levels. The top tier served as a walkway around the room and was lined with midnight blue wood flooring, Emya wondered if it was the natural color. Tables and chairs crowded the second level. Pale gold tablecloths were visible through the crystal plates and goblets, which were filled to the brim with wine or punch.

The third and lowest tier was filled with colorful dancers twirling and stomping across the vast, dark blue wood dancefloor to the magnificent symphony resonating through the room.

Overwhelmed by the grandeur, Emya clutched Felix for support as her legs threatened to collapse under her, causing him to stumble. A firm hand pried her off and wrapped around her arm, lending sturdy support. Emya glanced up; Artyem stared straight ahead, stone-faced.

Eventually, as they descended the steps to the tables, her stiff legs loosened and her churning mind calmed. Mr. and Mrs. Mellia waited for them at a table close to the stairs, which was a little apart from the other, giving it the appearance of being the center of the gathering. Evris and her family were already seated. At the indication of their hosts, they sat. Emya was next to Evris, Felix next to her, and Artyem was between Felix and Mr. Kabris, who looked eager to pester him with questions. Mrs. Kabris and their two other children filled the rest of the chairs.

As though bidden by some unseen signal, or perhaps they were just observant, the staff came around with trays of small plates with little treats. At first baffled by their way of serving food, Emya now knew better than to fill up on savory tarts and colorful arrangements of sliced fruit. Why they couldn't serve all the food at once she had no idea.

As expected, Mr. Kabris was pressing Artyem with so many questions that neither was eating. Felix seemed to only have eyes for the food, though he managed to maintain light conversation with Mrs. Kabris and her younger children, who were asking increasingly ridiculous questions about magic.

"Is it possible," Dini asked slowly, her face screwed up in thought, "to make a horse grow as big as a mountain?"

"Well," Felix said, suppressing a laugh. "It's possible, but very difficult and not necessarily a good idea."

"What about..." Breck asked, trying to one-up his sister. "Turning the whole ocean into whipped cream?"

Dini gasped and frowned.

"I was gonna ask that!" she cried.

Felix laughed. "No, I don't think that's really possible."

"But a horse as big as a mountain is?" Dini asked indignantly. Apparently, they were trying to see who could come up with the most impossible magical feat.

"What about making all our crops grow as much as possible?" Mrs. Kabris joined in, though she wasn't trying to surpass her children in ridiculousness.

"That's possible," Felix said. "Though the problem is that when done too often it can cause some adverse effects. We're not entirely sure how to prevent your carrots from coming alive and eating you in revenge."

The children gasped, wide-eyed and stunned, believing it wholly. Mrs. Kabris laughed heartily. Felix grinned. Though she knew he was joking, an unsettling tingle trembled down Emya's spine; after everything that had happened in her village, angry living vegetables wouldn't have surprised her.

Felix must have noticed her discomfort because he leaned over and whispered, "I'm joking. That can't happen."

Emya smiled and laughed a little, which seemed to satisfy him.

The music eventually hummed to a stop and everyone took their seats. Moments after the last guest was seated, servers laden with trays of steaming dishes appeared.

"Have you finished packing?" Evris asked. Emya hadn't. She had been planning on taking only what she brought, and that didn't require much packing, but now that she was to bring all the clothes she'd been given, she still had the task ahead of her.

"No," she said. "I'll have to do it tonight."

Evris grinned.

"I'm not finished either," she said. "I still have some clothes out to dry."

They grinned at their shared procrastination.

After stuffing herself with roast fish, potatoes and carrots, she managed to indulge in a dessert of chocolate cake, after which she could hardly move. As she slouched in her chair the music started up once more and Evris was on her feet.

"Come and dance," she said to Emya.

"No. I'd rather not," Emya said.

Evris shrugged and turned to Felix.

"Surely you dance."

He smiled. "I do. And I don't see the harm."

He took Evris by the hand, ignoring Artyem's skeptical look, and led her to the center of the dance floor where other guests were lining up for the dance. Evris turned just enough to give Emya the slyest of winks.

Felix was more graceful than Emya would have imagined when she first knew him. Dancing was not new to him, evidently; he stepped and turned in perfect timing.

Mr. Kabris, having exhausted all his curiosity, asked his wife to dance. Their children following behind them to join a group of other children in their own unbridled balter.

"Are there parties like this at Civim?" Emya asked Artyem.

"No," he said. "There are gatherings, but not quite like this."

"I can't believe there is anything like this anywhere else." Emya gestured to the room in general.

"There are," he said taking a sip of wine. "Much grander than this, too."

"I might like to see that someday," she said.

"You likely will if you become a mage. Many kings and leaders of men seek out the counsel and services of mages."

"Why?" Emya asked skeptically. "Who would want to deal in magic who did not have to?"

"Having second thoughts?" For a moment she saw pity in his expression, but it quickly changed to indifference.

"No," she said, blushing. "I didn't think people would seek out mages for any other purpose than to take magic for themselves. Not for the service of the mage."

Artyem scowled. "That seldom happens. Except in your case, it is not possible. To answer your question though, they want to use it to solve their more confounding problems. It is the duty of mage to judge how much magic can be used and how."

At that moment, one of the young ladies who always seemed to gravitate towards Artyem took the empty seat next to him.

"Still stubborn a man as ever," she said, laughing. "Won't you dance just this once?"

Artyem shook his head resolutely. "It is not in my nature. I'm afraid I have no sense of rhythm."

"Easily remedied. I'll lead," she said.

"I don't think so."

The young lady laughed and started up a conversation about some business with animals they'd obviously been having for some time. Artyem engaged in it with what for him could be considered enthusiasm, though Emya detected a hint of relief. Unable to contribute to the conversation, Emya got up to watch the dancing from a better vantage point.

Standing on the bottom step of the stair, she watched the complex twirling and stepping. As soon as she had worked out the pattern, the dance changed. It was grace and beauty from unfathomable chaos, and she could have watched it forever without the desire to join in. Evris was especially graceful, her smiling face flushed as she followed the motions of her partner with perfect timing.

The music was lively and fast-paced, but as it changed to a slow, quiet melody a tall figure sidled up beside her and held out a hand. She turned her gaze to Felix, flushed and sweaty, his eyes alight and eager. He looked the most alive she'd ever seen him; unrecognizable from the broken boy she'd met not so long ago.

"This is an easy one, I'll show you," he said. Then, seeing her apprehension, he added, "It'll be fun, I promise. We can stop if you don't like it."

They'd been through so many horrible things together, it was time to do something enjoyable. She could try it, for him.

Timidly, she took his hand and let him lead her to the edge of the dancers. He showed her the basic steps and led her in a simple dance of rising and falling, weaving through the other dancers in a spiraling pattern. Tension released with every step. Felix's hands pressed against her palm and shoulder as he gently led her through the steps. He only smiled when she stepped on his toes and laughed at her surprise when he twirled her under his arm in the center of the spiral. The music hummed to a stop and everyone clapped, leaving the dance floor. Emya started to follow them, but Felix held her back. Artyem and Evris came to stand next to them. The guests surrounded them. Evris' family was front and center, smiling proudly at their daughter. Mr. and Mrs. Mellia ambled over, arm in arm, and turned to address the party.

"We thank you all for coming," Mr. Mellia said. "Tonight, we say farewell to these three wonderful people we've had the pleasure to stay with us."

There were calls of agreement and encouragement. Mr. Mellia silenced them with a hand.

"It is a particularly special occasion when we have the pleasure to host our dear friend Artyem." General sounds of agreement followed this. "But it was a wonderful surprise to be able to have Felix come to stay with us, who, as you know, does not visit often enough."

Cries of mock scorn and condemnation filled the room. Felix waved sheepishly, though he could not hide a mischievous grin.

"And, of course, my wife and I have had the great privilege of getting to know Miss Emya. We have discovered that she is a kind, thoughtful, intelligent, and all-around pleasant girl. We will miss having her and we wish her the best in her journey."

Exuberant applause interjected with well-wishes and cheers filled the room. Emya covered her burning face and peeked through her fingers. The noise died down quickly, as Mr. Mellia must have seen the tears threatening to overwhelm her. When Mrs. Mellia wrapped her in a crushing hug, Emya buried her face in her shoulder. Being held by the kind woman gave her the comfort to compose herself. The wide smile Emya had was genuine, and when she broke away Mrs. Mellia surreptitiously wiped her own cheeks.

"You are all most welcome here at any time," Mr. Mellia went on when there was quiet once more. "And now..."

He drew Evris away from the group to stand before the crowd. "As a few of you know, and many of you have guessed, the true purpose for the visit of an emissary of Civim. I am delighted to announce that our dear Evris Kabris will be leaving tomorrow to study magic at Civim."

Emya's heart went cold for the space of a breath. Then raucous applause filled the room, followed by cheers of delight and congratulations. Several men reached over to shake her father's hand, and Evris's friends shouted, "I knew it!"

Evris, elated beyond measure, grinned at her parents and shouted good-natured abuse at her friends. When the noise died down Mr. Mellia continued, addressing Evris. "We are all extremely proud of you and the task you are about the undertake. We look forward to watching you grow and become the best mage you can be. And, as a token of our appreciation," he paused before taking a delicate silver chain with a small crystal star pendant and presented it to Evris. "The treasure of your ancestor, Vridis."

Evris took the necklace to the sound of more formal applause. Emya looked sideways at Felix and Artyem and saw the same look of surprise and impression. The gift was more significant than it appeared.

"And so," Mr. Mellia concluded, addressing the four of them, "We wish you a safe journey."

With that, the party broke up. The guests thanked their hosts and headed towards the doors. Evris ran to her parents and friends who hugged her and clamored for her attention. Several people came to greet Artyem and Felix and wish them a safe journey, hoping to see them again soon. Emya stood back, trying not to be noticed, but Evris appeared and took her by the arm, leading her to her family so they could hug her.

Eventually, she found herself in the foyer, saying goodnight to the last of the guests. Artyem chatted with the young woman who'd been at his side all night. Mr. And Mrs. Kabris were taking a while to say goodnight to Felix and Mr. and Mrs. Mellia.

"I'll see you in the morning," Evris said. "I'm so excited I don't think I'll be able to sleep."

"You had better try though," Emya said. "You don't want to be too tired to hike up a mountain."

"Well you'd know, wouldn't you?" Evris said, "I'll try to sleep, but so must you."

Emya promised she would sleep. Unlike Evris, she was exhausted and felt no excitement for the journey ahead. She was still very apprehensive about the trip, and if it was anything like her journey through the Red Forest, it was nothing to be excited about—though she wasn't going to tell that to Evris. Before she had a chance to ask her why she would know about hiking, Mrs. Kabris herded her family out the door.

The Mellia's said goodnight to Emya and Felix. Along with Artyem, who'd managed to see off his female friend with a certain amount of persuasion, Felix and Emya climbed the stairs.

"It's not going to be an easy trek," Artyem said as they reached her room. "Make sure you get some sleep."

"I'm sure she will, she looks tired," Felix said.

"I am and I will," Emya assured him.

"Good, but I was talking to Felix," Artyem replied.

Felix turned with a scathing retort, but Artyem was already walking away. Felix shook his head.

"Well goodnight, Emya. Sleep well."

"Goodnight," she said.

Felix hurried off after Artyem. With a little shake of her head, she entered her room. Candles burned on the nightstand and window ledge, illuminating the room in just enough warm light for her to see the nightdress laid out and a pot of fragrant herbal tea. Pouring some into the accompanying mug, she sat on the bed, sipping the delicate mint and dandelion tea. She contemplated the closet door and how much energy she had left for packing. In the end, she decided it could wait until morning. Undressing and carefully hanging her beautiful dress up in the closet, she pulled on the nightgown.

Eyelids heavy and warmed from the tea, she fell into bed. As she drifted into the semiconscious directly preceding sleep, a strange feeling came over her. It was a mixture of fear, anger, and pain. She felt it acutely, but at the same time, she could not quite describe the way it coursed through her as though it was a foreign substance, a poison. It was not like the companion, which latched onto the part of her that dealt with magic

122

but otherwise did not interfere. This oozed through her, tightening her muscles, squeezing her heart and lungs. She gasped for air. Trapped by her own paralyzed muscles, she could not yell out for help as inky black overtook her.

"Emya!"

Someone shook her. Immediately her muscles relaxed, her heart beat out a rapid tattoo in her chest. Her vision, at first fuzzy in the dim light, cleared. Felix's face glowed in the candlelight, concern etched in his shadowed features. Emya blinked and sat up. He looked as pale and shaky as she felt.

"What is it?" she mumbled. "What happened?"

"I'm not sure yet," he said, sitting on the edge of her bed. "I was talking to Artyem and..." He looked down at his hands, obscuring his face in shadow. "He was trying to convince me to wait a little longer. The way he said it, sounded the way the Kings used to speak to me."

Emya leaned forward. Ever since he'd started to recover, he'd not spoken of his time with the Kings. He twisted his hands in his lap and Emya resisted the urge to take them in her own. She wanted to still them as to still her own nerves.

"Just for a moment, barely a phrase," he said. "I know he didn't mean it. I got angry and afraid. I lost the shred of control I had on my magic."

He sighed and opened up the drawer of the nightstand where the companion was stowed. Emya hadn't told him it was there.

"I felt this." He held up the black orb, a void in the candlelight. "It tried to take it all. My magic. I lashed out, attempting to save my life, and I think I hurt you through this."

In silence, they stared at the object for several minutes. The candle flickered although the air was still.

"It's alright," Emya said at last. "I'm alright. But

what if it happens again?"

"For now, it won't." He sighed deeply, his shoulders sagging. The shadow of his self with the Kings seeping through. "It's sapped my magic. It's too weak for me to use. I am as powerless as I was when the Kings drained me."

"But it will strengthen, won't it?"

"Eventually, though it would be dishonest not to admit that I need the skills of the healers in Civim. I still have the strength to travel, and Artyem agrees, grudgingly, that we must go now, lest I should backslide."

Emya nodded. "And you're sure the companion can't take what little is left of your magic?"

A grim smiled played across his pale lips.

"No, I am not."

PART TWO
WINDING EVER HIGHER

BIO

As a young girl Amy enjoyed hearing the tales of
Redwall and Harry Potter read to her by her mother
every night. As a result, she brings her lifelong love of
fantasy to life in her writing. With a degree in Molecular
Biology she also has a love for science and science
fiction. When she is not writing she is knitting, going to
the beach, or spending time with her family.